Girls Gone Magic

Christina F. York

Girls Gone Magic
Christina F. York

Print edition published 2014 by Tsunami Ridge.

"Sharper Than A Serpent's Tooth" first published in *Hags, Sirens, and Other Bad Girls of Fantasy*, ed. Denise Little, DAW Books, 2006.

"Cupid's Crib" first published in *Enchantment Place*, ed. Denise Little, DAW Books, 2008.

"Cheer Witches" first published as "Perfect Ten" in *Witch High*, ed. Denise Little, DAW Books, 2008.

"A Day at the Unicorn Races" first published in *Fantasy Gone Wrong*, ed. Martin S. Greenberg and Brittany A. Koren, DAW Books, 2006.

First Edition
ISBN-13: 978-0692287422
ISBN-10: 0692287426

Inquiries should be addressed to
Tsunami Ridge Publishing
RobotCEO@TsunamiRidge.com
TsunamiRidge.com

Cover image © -Misha / Fotalia

Praise for Christina F. York

"Finding a Chris York short story is like finding a gem in the rough. There are never enough of them. Now many of those gems of short stories found their way to this wonderful volume. Treasure and enjoy the read. I know I did."

—Dean Wesley Smith
USA Today bestselling author

"Reading Chris York is like curling up by the fire with an old friend. I know I'm going to have a good time."

—Phaedra Weldon
National bestselling author

"Components for a spellbinding short story collection: A keen eye for men's and women's foibles, from teens to senior citizens, especially when dealing with each other. Add a wry sense of humor and a unique way of looking at the world, whether from the perspective of a fairy-tale stepmother or a cheerleader in a school for magic-users. Combine all of these with an inimitable voice, and let Christina York's enchanting short fiction lead you on a journey to fantastical places from which you will not want to return."

—John Helfers
Editor of *How to Save the World*
and *Recycled Pulp* (Fiction River)

Also by Christina F. York

Novels

Dory Cove
Dream House
Loaves and Kisses
Rodeo Royalty

Writing as Christy Evans

Sink Trap
Lead Pipe Cinch
Drip Dead

Writing as Christy Fifield

Murder Buys a T-Shirt
Murder Hooks a Mermaid
Murder Sends a Postcard
Murder Ties the Knot

Short Stories

"Food Fight"
"Fortress of Solitude"
"Godspeed"

Table of Contents

Girls Gone
Magic

Christina F. York

Introduction

MAGIC MEANS SOMETHING different to everyone. Some people instantly imagine mythical creatures, or youngsters in swirling robes wielding wands and chanting incantations.

But to some magic describes the indefinable something that happens when two people meet, or the unbreakable link forged between parent and child. To others it represents the skills or talents of someone they admire, or envy.

For me, magic comes from the power that resides within each of us. I believe we can each tap into something special and, yes, magical. That power, for good or evil, can shape our lives and the lives of the people around us.

In these stories I looked for the magic in the lives of girls—and women—and how that magic shapes their lives. They are the stories of all of us.

Enjoy!

—*Christina F. York*

Sharper Than a Serpent's Tooth

Sharper Than a Serpent's Tooth

THEY SAY THAT HISTORY is written by the victors. Take it from one of the vanquished, truer words were never spoken.

Seriously, if that willful little girl hadn't become the queen, don't you think the story just might have been told a little differently?

But she did marry the prince, and eventually she became the queen. The Brothers Grimm—palace apologists, both of them—turned her story inside out and made her the heroine of the tale.

Don't get me wrong, she wasn't all bad, either, but I think it's time we set the record straight, in the name of justice for stepparents everywhere.

Being anyone's second wife isn't an easy task, and it's even harder if the first wife died tragically, surrounded by her loving family. No matter what you do, you're going to spend the rest of your life in that shadow.

Not that I'm bitter, mind you, because I'm really not.

I just want a little respect, is all.

If I had known, before I married the duke, the way things would end…well, I would have married him anyway.

There weren't many career paths for a widow with two daughters, after all. The only job skills I had involved husband-catching, and when my first husband died, I tightened my corset and set about finding another.

I had my daughters to take care of.

The night I met the duke was magical. The royal palace—we met at a royal ball—was lit by thousands of candles, hanging from chandeliers, standing between the platters on the heavy wooden banquet tables, and tucked into niches cut into the stone walls. Despite the chill in the outside air, the ballroom felt warm in the candlelight.

That night I thought the musicians must be angels, their music too beautiful to be the product of mere mortals. Mutton tasted like ambrosia. The men were more handsome, the women more beautiful, than any I had seen.

Clearly, I was smitten.

I really thought I had met the partner of my dreams, and when he made me his wife, I would be his other half. He promised to consult me, to heed my advice, and to be a father to my poor, orphaned daughters, Catherine and Anne.

Not that I'm bitter, mind you. I just want people to know the truth.

He made a lot of promises.

So, I married him, and the girls and I left my late husband's family home. Just as well, since his brother had taken over.

I had gone from running the household and supervising the estate and the tenant farmers to being a barely-tolerated interloper. My former in-laws were a real piece of work, I can tell you, but that's another story.

When I met my new daughter (the whole step-daughter thing came later, and it wasn't my idea, you know), I saw past her red-rimmed eyes and unkempt appearance. She had been without a mother for two years, and the duke didn't know how to care for a child.

She just needed someone to take care of her.

What I saw, underneath the tangled hair and dirty clothes, was a bright intelligence and an instinct for survival.

I should have been wary of both, but my heart went out to this little waif-child with the forlorn look. I may have been a sucker, but this kid had potential.

With the right training, she could run the kingdom.

That much, at least, I got right.

My girls, I'm afraid, suffered by comparison. Oh, they were both very pretty, just like I was at their ages. They knew how to dress well, as long as there was enough money for seamstresses and shoemakers, and how to supervise a household staff. They were graceful dancers and could carry on with the kind of pleasantries that said nothing and offended no one.

They would make very good wives someday.

* * *

Within days of moving into the castle, I began to see how badly things had been let go after the duke's first wife died. Not only had Cynthia, my new daughter, been neglected, but the castle had been allowed to run down, and the servants had become a rebellious, slovenly lot.

I thought my husband could use some help.

Our first argument, prophetically enough, was about Cynthia.

"She should be better dressed," I said.

"Why? She spends most of her time with the cook in the kitchen; she'd only ruin anything better." The duke shoveled in another pile of turnips and glared at me.

I tried to appeal to his parental pride. "But she's a lovely child. She should have clothes that are as pretty as she is."

They say clothes make the man, and that goes double, of maybe triple, for women. You have to dress the part, and she was wearing servant's rags.

"Dress her as you will," the duke said, waving a hand at me. "Just be careful of your spending. I'm not made of money, you know."

I hesitated, but he had promised to heed my advice. "I'll see that she gets proper clothes. And there are ways your estate could be more profitable. Perhaps we could talk about it. Later."

I gave him what I thought was a seductive smile. We were newlyweds, after all, and that should have made him happy.

My mistake.

"I doubt I'll need the help of a woman to make my estate profitable. Tend to the household, like a good wife, and leave the rest to me."

He bent over his plate, effectively cutting off any chance of discussion. It was the first time he had dismissed me so quickly, but it was far from the last.

* * *

Cynthia wasn't any easier to deal with than her father.

I called her to my chamber the next day, where I waited with a truck of clothes my older girls had outgrown.

"Cynthia, come look at what I have here."

I tried to be as nonthreatening as I could. I didn't intend to replace her mother. Really, I didn't. I just wanted to help.

But you can't help some people.

"Your father and I are going to order you some new dresses." I tried not to look at the gray rags she wore, stained with soot and God-knows-what from the kitchen.

"But the dressmakers will need some time to get them ready. In the meantime, I thought you might find something in here you would like."

My late husband had never denied his girls anything, and that truck was packed with gorgeous clothes. Silks and laces, fine brocades, in rich blues and greens. They were more suited to my fair-haired older girls than to this dark-eyed youngster, but they were beautiful clothes.

Cynthia refused to look in the trunk. She wouldn't try on any of the dresses, and she clung stubbornly to her ragged skirt and tunic. "These are my clothes," she said. "I have no need of charity."

"They aren't charity, child. They're just clothes your sisters have outgrown."

I tried to get closer, the way you try to sidle up to a wary animal, but she was having none of it.

"They aren't my sisters. And you aren't my mother!"

She ran out of my chamber and refused to leave her room for three days. Of course the servants sided with her, smuggling food in to her, and warning her every time I came by.

I know the story claims she had no clothes besides that single ragged skirt and tunic, but the truth is, there was an entire room filled with the work of seamstresses.

I think they were eventually given to charity.

* * *

So there I was. My so-called job skills had captured another husband, but he wasn't the man I thought he was. His idea of consulting me was to ask what I wanted cook to prepare for lunch. Not dinner—that was always his choice.

As for being a father to my daughters, he figured if there was food on the table and a roof overhead, he was good.

I watched my three daughters growing up.

Catherine and Anne would marry well enough and be content with their lots.

Cynthia, though, was too stubborn for her own good.

She still wouldn't wear the clothes I had made for her, and she continued to sleep in the kitchen. Not that I blamed her for that. It was the only place in the entire castle that was warm, and there were nights I would have joined her, but I didn't dare. She was the only one the cook would tolerate.

She was always the darling of the servants.

* * *

When the invitation came for the prince's ball, the entire household fell apart.

Catherine and Anne were absolutely convinced they would catch the prince's eye, and they fought between themselves constantly over which one would be queen.

I thought their chances were good—they had been well-trained—but I knew the competition would be fierce.

We spent long days preparing for the big night.

I invited Cynthia to join us. "You could attend the ball," I said. "We could go as a family."

Wrong thing to say.

"I'm not part of your family," she said. Like I said, she was a stubborn child, and she had long ago decided we weren't related.

The older girls were fitted for their gowns. They practiced walking and curtsying in their new shoes and fussed over their jewelry and hair. This was their chance to capture the heart of the prince.

There were times when I knew Cynthia was eavesdropping on us as we prepared.

I would hear steps outside my chamber or in the gallery above the hall where the girls practiced their dance steps. When I turned to look, all I could see was the tail of a tattered gray skirt.

But I knew she was listening.

I'm sure Catherine and Anne thought I had lost my mind, when I talked to them about ambition, since neither of them suffered from an abundance.

But they weren't my real audience.

* * *

The night of the ball arrived, and Cynthia still refused to attend with us. She claimed that she had nothing fit to wear, as if that were my fault.

I considered, for just a moment, staying home with her, and trying, one last time, to get through to her. But then I looked at Catherine and Anne, dressed and waiting. At least I could help them.

Wrong again.

* * *

We arrived in front of the castle in the middle of a long line of carriages. Footmen, decked out in their finest livery, helped us down from our coach and onto the carpet rolled out on the broad stone steps. At the door, a herald announced each arrival.

The main ballroom was a swirl of light and color. Candles flickered everywhere, as they had the night I met the duke. The light reflected from satin gowns in every color of the rainbow and glinted off lavish displays of jewels.

Every woman of marriageable age in the land was there. Except Cynthia, of course.

There was a feast spread across the banquet tables. The aroma of roast beef mingled with the sweet musk of mulled wine, and piles of honey-drizzled cakes added the smell of clover.

It was more spectacular than I could have imagined, and Catherine and Anne were quickly caught up in the dancing, as I watched from the edge of the room.

I had taught them all I could. Now all I could do was watch.

They were doing just fine, and Catherine was next on the prince's dance card, when trouble appeared at the door in the form of a dark-haired beauty dressed in an exquisite gown of rose-colored satin and dainty gold slippers.

The men, all of them, stared, and the herald wasn't even able to speak her name. She glided into the room on those gold slippers, and the prince abandoned Catherine to rush to her side.

He never left her side, and danced with her the rest of the evening. We all knew his search was over.

In one way, it was better for Anne. I saw her dancing with a rather dashing young count, and she was clearly practicing those husband-catching job skills. She would be fine.

The wine flowed, the music played, and the prince danced with his new-found love. The king and queen looked on, obviously pleased their son had found someone.

It looked like happily ever after was just around the corner.

Until the clock began to strike midnight.

The beautiful stranger—we never had heard her name—tore herself away from the prince and ran for the door. He ran after her, yelling for his guards to stop her, but she dodged them.

She didn't stop, didn't even say good-bye. She ran out of the castle, leaving behind one tiny gold slipper.

* * *

The prince searched the entire kingdom, looking for the woman who fit that gold slipper. It was small and delicate, and there weren't many girls who could even come close to wearing it.

No matter how they tried, neither Catherine nor Anne could fit more than a couple toes into it.

I think Anne was actually relieved, since the count she had met at the ball had already begun to court her, but Catherine was disappointed.

The search party was ready to leave our castle when Cynthia came out of the kitchen. She just stood in the corner, near the fire, but the prince caught sight of her and looked back and forth between her and the duke.

"My daughter," the duke said. "But she didn't attend the ball. She can't be the girl you're looking for."

The prince insisted, and of course the slipper fit.

I knew it would.

The prince wanted Cynthia to accompany him to the castle immediately, and she quickly agreed.

"I have searched for days to find you," he told her, "and I can't live without you another day."

Cynthia looked at me, smiling. It was the last time she spoke directly to me.

"A smart woman disguises her ambition."

* * *

Cynthia married the prince, of course. I knew all along that she would, since it was the only way she could run the kingdom. And no matter what she says, she learned a lot from me. Of course, she has the prince—he's the king now—so completely enchanted that he lets her do pretty much whatever she wants.

I like to think of that as my legacy.

As for me, I have a little place in the countryside. Her Highness takes care of the bills and leaves me alone. I think she expects me to stay here and keep her secrets, and for the most part that's what I've done.

But before I die, I wanted to tell the whole story.

I'm not bitter. Really.

A Day at the Unicorn Races

A Day at the Unicorn Races

ALPHONSE LISTENED to the track announcer calling the end of the Meadowland Stakes race, as he watched from the rail. The thunder of hooves shook the ground under his feet, and dust assailed his nose, as the racers passed his position.

Fairy Dust was one of his favorites, even though trainers weren't supposed to have favorites.

And Bubbles, the jockey, was one of his favorites, too. He probably shouldn't have favorite jockeys, either, but screw that. She looked good in the silks, and he could imagine what she would look like out of them. Hell, he'd even had a preview or two in the changing rooms, even though the women's locker was supposed to be off limits to men.

But Bubbles didn't feature having him in her life, not by a long shot. Not as long as she was a unicorn racer. Just his luck to fall for a woman with a career that didn't leave much room for romance.

It wasn't like he hadn't tried. He'd done all the polite things, made all the non-threatening moves he knew.

Both of them.

But she'd been pretty clear. He couldn't find a good answer to "Get your damned hands off of me." She might be little, but dainty wasn't a word that described Bubbles.

Fairy Dust was moving along the rail, challenging for the lead, with only a few seconds left in the race. He seemed to respond to the screaming of the crowd, putting on a last-second burst of speed, and moving into a photo finish.

While the crowd buzzed, waiting for the results, Alphonse slipped through the gate into the paddock, where the mounts were cooling down.

As a trainer, he was one of the few people allowed near the unicorns. Only virgins could ride, but fortunately trainers didn't have to be quite so pure. He'd thought about being a jockey once, but that whole no-sex-thing had changed his mind. Who wanted to voluntarily spend the rest of his life in a constant state of frustration?

Bubbles was still astride Fairy Dust, leaning forward over his neck, stroking his horn, and whispering in his ear.

Alphonse suddenly wished he was a unicorn.

As she stroked the horn, Bubbles stood up slightly in her saddle, leaning forward. The tight silk of her riding pants stretched across her trim bottom.

Was the woman deliberately torturing him?

Bubbles glanced around the paddock, catching sight of Alphonse. Her eyes were bright with the excitement of the race, and a little unfocused, her face flushed. She smiled at Alphonse, and nudged Fairy Dust toward him.

Sliding from the saddle, Bubbles dropped down next to Alphonse. "Did you see the son-of-a-bitch run?" She was buzzing with adrenaline. "Did you see?"

Before Alphonse could reply, the finish photo flashed on the tote board. Fairy Dust, muscles straining, had pushed his horn ahead of the number two finisher, by a fraction of an inch.

Bubbles cheered, and jumped into Alphonse's arms, wrapping her slender legs around his waist, and kissing him lustily.

For an instant, they were both in the moment, in the kiss, passion and desire flowing freely.

Then Bubbles broke the kiss and dropped to the ground. Her face clouded, and frustration instantly replaced passion.

"Dammit!" She stomped away. "Don't do that to me!"

As she moved off, Alphonse could hear a string of muttered curses. He shook his head.

She was trying to torture him.

* * *

The jockey's changing room was a miasma of steam and sweat, the clash of a dozen different soap and shampoo scents creating a stomach-churning cloud of olfactory overload.

Bubbles shoved her way to her locker, shooting dirty looks at anyone who crossed her part.

"Watch out," called a tiny woman wrapped in a towel. "Bubbles is horny. Again!"

"Am not!" Bubbles shot back.

The retort was greeted with a wave of laughter from all over the room.

"You sooo are too," the woman replied. She stopped in front of a locker with the name "Rainbow" stenciled on the front, and pulled out a small silver flask. "Here," she tossed it to Bubbles, "drown your sorrows."

Bubbles tilted her head back and took a long swallow from the flask before tossing it back to Rainbow. "I don't need to drown my sorrows, but I am not about to pass up free gin."

"Honey," Rainbow said, stowing the flask back in her locker, "it may just be time to hang up your silks."

"Bullshit." Bubbles stripped off the garments in question, and tossed them in a basket for cleaning. "Never happen."

"Listen to you, acting all tough," called Sunshine from the next bank of lockers. "Keep this up, you're gonna explode, I swear it."

"You never swear, Sunny. And I am not even going to dignify that with an answer," Bubbles said. She wrapped a rough towel around her, and marched off to the shower.

Maybe a cold shower would just wash away the frustration.

It wasn't that she didn't like Alphonse well enough. Hell, if she wasn't a jockey, she might even give him a tumble, but it would mean losing her job, her career, and for what?

As Bubbles dressed, Rainbow and Sunshine continued to taunt her. Finally, when all three were leaving the locker room, Rainbow threw a friendly arm over Bubbles' shoulder.

"You aren't the only one, you know," she whispered confidentially. "We've all thought about it."

"No shit. Like that's a big surprise."

"No, really," Sunshine said, earnestly. "We do think about it. How can you not?"

"But there's nothing we can do about it. Not if we want to keep our jobs. One little tumble, and poof!" Bubbles waved her hands. "Remember Tatiana? She had some scheme that was supposed to fool Angel Heart."

Sunshine's big blue eyes grew wide, and a single, perfect tear formed in one corner. "That poor girl! She was in the hospital for months when he threw her!"

Bubbles snorted in disgust. "Well, duh! Thought she could fool a unicorn? Hello! Magical creatures here, not gonna be fooled by some bimbo with a hormone overload."

Rainbow patted Bubbles on the back, as the three women made their way into the now-deserted parking lot. "You try to act like you're all hard-hearted and don't care, but we know better, Bubby. And we know Alphonse is pretty sweet on you, too."

Sunshine's mouth turned down at the corners, and she cocked her head to the side. "It's all sad and tragic, you know. Throwing away all that for a job."

"It's not all that, it's just a little roll in hay. Literally, if Tatiana is any example. And it's way more than a job, anyway," Bubbles shot back. "It's like my entire life. Racing is everything."

Rainbow's ancient Honda, painted in rainbow colors, and covered with decals from all the tracks they had visited, sat in the far corner of the lot.

The three women piled in, and Rainbow headed for The Finish Line, the local track hangout.

At a table in the jockey's corner, they had a beer, and the conversation picked up where it had left off.

They were nearly shouting over the din in the bar, the blaring jukebox providing a base for the buzz of conversation, punctuated by occasional shrill, alcohol-fueled laughter.

"I say go for it." Rainbow was not going to let it drop.

Bubbles shook her head. "Do I look like I am insane? Even if I am hot for his frame—which I am not, thank you very much—but even if I was, what am I gonna do? Throw away my entire life?"

"For love?" Sunshine asked, dreamily. "I can't think of a better reason." She sighed, a drawn-out, dramatic exhalation. "It must be wonderful to have someone love you."

"Sunny, get a grip! I don't love Al." Bubbles turned to glare at Rainbow. "And I am not hot for him, either."

Rainbow raised a skeptical eyebrow, but she didn't argue.

Across the bar, Alphonse watched Bubbles. She hadn't seen him when she came in, and he knew better than to approach a jockey in The Finish Line. The women jockey's corner was strictly off-limits to men.

She was a lost cause. Every time he got close to her, she turned as prickly as a cactus, all sharp points and attitude to spare.

That was the thing about the jockeys. They might be virgins, but they weren't all sweetness-and-light, oh no, not by a long shot. Most of 'em were kind of nasty when you got right down to it.

So why was he still watching Bubbles sip her beer?

Maybe he was the lost cause.

* * *

Bubbles paced the floor of her apartment. It was late, but she had a beer buzz, and she didn't want to sleep.

She stomped through the tiny area she laughingly called a living room, sidestepping her broken-down recliner, and dodging a basket of unfolded laundry.

She tried not to think about Al, about how it felt when she kissed him. Well, duh! She might be a rider—a virgin—but it didn't mean she was dead or something. Everything worked just fine, thank you.

She glanced at the kitchen, a wall of counters with a miniature refrigerator, a two-burner cook top, and a single sink piled with dirty dishes. Not that she needed anything more elaborate. Had to stay at her racing weight, after all.

She yanked open the refrigerator door, wondering if, by some miracle, she had a beer hidden in there, and glared at the contents. Some wilted salad, a take-out container from Wong Lee's—steamed rice and broccoli—that she couldn't remember ordering. No beer.

Probably a good thing. It would mean an extra hour in the gym, sweating off the calories that came with the cold, golden goodness that came in that can. Even a light beer—yuck!—would cost her.

She slammed the refrigerator door, the thought of a beer reminding her of the conversation in the Finish Line. Her parts worked just fine, she just chose not to use some of them. It was a personal decision. Someday she might change her mind, but for now, some things were just more important than sex.

Oh, Sunshine would insist Bubbles was in love with Al, which was so totally not true. And Rainbow would tell her everybody had to hang it up sometime, that nobody raced forever, and there were other things she could do.

What did they know?

She growled, wishing they were here so she could tell them how wrong they were. She was so not ready to quit racing. She loved the excitement of the race, the feeling that she got when she rode a winner. She even enjoyed the feeling of being in Alphonse's arms, and the tinglies that came from kissing him.

But kissing would lead to more, and more would lead to even more, and before she knew it, she could be out of racing, and thinking about a second career.

No. Better she didn't even start down that road.

She paced back through the living room, slammed her fist against a lumpy cushion that sat in the recliner, and stomped into the bathroom. She needed another cold shower.

* * *

In the changing room, the jockeys were in the usual state of pre-race jitters. Rainbow was standing in front of her locker, fingering her assortment of lucky charms, including the four-leaf clover she had found on a recent picnic.

Rainbow hadn't said much about it, but Bubbles knew it involved a man, and the clover had become a talisman for Rainbow. Judging by the goofy smile on her face, there was a girl who was getting ready to hang up her silks.

Not Bubbles.

Bubbles' talisman, if you could call it that, was a battered jockey's cap she had picked up after Angel Heart had thrown Tatiana. Every time she looked at it, she was reminded of Tatiana, who had tried to have it all.

And look where that got her. She slammed the door on the cap, her resolve stiffening her spine.

"Take it easy."

Bubbles looked up to find Sunshine looking at her pityingly, her big blue eyes round and solemn.

"What is your problem?" Bubbles growled.

Sunshine just shook her head. Rainbow turned, her face an angry red. "Could you both just keep it down? Some of us have to work today! Just because your boyfriend gives you the best runners, Bubby, doesn't give you the right to screw with the rest of us."

Bubbles sighed with disgust. "He is not my boyfriend. And I get the rides I deserve." She waved a hand in dismissal. "Whatever. Just get over your attitude before you get out on the track."

Bubbles turned her back on Rainbow, and caught Sunshine's wide eyes. She hooked a thumb over her shoulder, in Rainbow's direction. "I think we know who's horny today," she muttered.

"Take that back!"

Rainbow was on her in a flash, all elbows and bony fingers, digging into Bubbles unpadded ribs.

Bubbles went down, with Rainbow astride her, pinning her to the cold concrete floor of the changing room.

"Take it back!"

Bubbles bit her lip and refused to speak. Rainbow was constantly on her ass about Al. It was about time she had a dose of her own medicine.

"I swear, Bubbles, I don't have to take this—"

Rainbow was jerked backwards, her words cut off, her face shocked.

Behind her, Bubbles could see Sunshine, tears streaming down her face. "Stop it!" she screamed. "Both of you, just stop it! I can't stand it when you fight."

Bubbles climbed slowly to her feet, brushing off her silks. Though the floor was clean, the gesture gave her a minute to collect herself.

She gave Rainbow a hard look, then turned her attention to Sunny. She had stopped crying, but her nose was red and swollen, and her eyes were puffy.

Bubbles felt instantly contrite for upsetting Sunny, even if Rainbow was acting like a jerk. "Sorry, Sunny. But you have to admit, she was being a bitch."

Rainbow was back on her feet, the color high in her cheeks, and her breathing fast. She took a step toward Bubbles, lifting her fists in front of her, then shook her head and backed away.

"Aw, hell!" she said, slapping her locker shut. The clang of metal-on-metal echoed off the bare walls of the room. "You may be right." She turned around to face Bubbles. "But it takes one to know one."

Rainbow stamped away, the sound of her boots clicking against the concrete fading as she disappeared through the door to the paddock.

Sunshine stared after her, her face troubled. "Oh, Bubby," she wailed. "I don't think I've ever seen her that way."

Bubbles sat down on the hard bench in front of her locker. "Neither have I, Sunny. Ever."

Bubbles winced as a thought struck her. "I don't act like that, do I? I mean, you guys are on me all the time, and I was just dishing it back. But I'm not like that."

"Well," Sunshine dropped down onto the bench beside Bubbles, and slipped her arm around her friend's narrow shoulders. "You do get a little crabby now and then. Especially when you've been around Al. Not that it's all that bad," she added hastily, as Bubbles tensed. "Not really that bad at all. Just sometimes …"

Her voice trailed off, and she drew back. "No, not that bad." She stood quickly, her voice suddenly brisk and unemotional. "I better go make sure Rainbow's okay."

* * *

The last race of the day was a big one, and Bubbles was up on Fairy Dust again. The two of them seemed to understand each other, and riding him was usually a pure joy.

But today wasn't one of those days. As they broke from the gate, he surged into the lead, refusing her attempts to slow him down, to set the pace for their run.

Again and again, Fairy Dust fought her control. He would not hold back, wouldn't let the other runners tire themselves out. Instead, he forced himself faster and faster with each length.

Bubbles could feel him beginning to tire. His stride wasn't as sure, and when another unicorn pulled up on the inside, he hesitated before trying to cut him off.

Bubbles felt a surge of disappointment, then anger, as Foo Foo Fifi went by on her left, Sunshine hunched over his neck, urging him on.

She raised her whip, a tactic she almost never used on Fairy Dust, pushed herself forward, flattening her body against the big animal's neck.

"Run, you son-of-a-bitch!" she shouted, tapping him lightly on the flank with her whip. She didn't need to hit him, never had needed the whip, and she wasn't about to start now.

But she wasn't about to lose, either.

She felt Fairy Dust falter again, then he regained his footing, and his stride steadied.

Then began to pull ahead of the pack, leaving the rest of the racers behind. All except Sunshine and Fifi.

They rounded the last turn, the two racers so close that the announcer had fallen momentarily silent. There was no way to say who was in the lead.

The finish line was straight ahead, and neither unicorn was giving an inch.

In the last five lengths, with the rest of the field bearing down on them, Fifi stumbled. He brushed against Fairy Dust, and for one sickening moment, Bubbles thought they were going down.

Instead, Sunshine pulled up on her mount, taking him closer to the rail, and out of the path of Bubbles and Fairy Dust.

It was over in an instant. Fairy Dust flashed across finish line, with Fifi a length behind.

Relief flowed through Bubbles. She had won, despite her ride's erratic behavior. This was what it was all about.

Bubbles let the reins lay slack against the unicorn's neck. She stood easily in the stirrups, leaning forward to pat her racing partner. They were a good team, even if he was acting peculiar today.

Then Fairy Dust reared, his front feet pawing the air. He snorted once, and twisted beneath her.

Bubble's stomach dropped with a sickening wrench, as her feet left the stirrups, and she went flying through the air.

She landed on her back, on the hard-packed dirt of the track, her breath knocked from her lungs, and one leg twisted beneath her.

For one long, agonizing moment, she was afraid to move. Broken bones were a fact of the racing life, and she'd had her share. Still, they weren't her idea of a good time.

She stirred, but before she could sit up, the medics were at her side, forcing her back down. They poked and prodded for long minutes, before they would let her up.

She struggled into a sitting position on the hard ground. Waiting behind the medics were her crew: Sunshine, tears welling in her eyes—that girl cried for anything!—and Rainbow.

And beside them was Al. Dear, sweet Al. Who had put her up on a mount that damn near killed her.

"What the hell is his problem?" she stormed at Al.

His eyes widened, and he took a small step back, but then he seemed to sort of mentally shake himself, and he moved up close to her.

"His problem? Nothing much. Except that filly that was in the barn earlier today. Got him all riled up."

Al ran his eyes over her. Her silks were dusty and twisted around from the medic's inspection. Her helmet was askew, hanging over one ear and uncovering a serious case of helmet hair. Her face was covered with a light coat of dust, and there was a bruise already developing on one pale cheek.

She was beautiful.

"And I know exactly how he feels."

Al held out his hand, and she let him pull her to her feet. Nothing like a little brush with mortality to make a girl realize what was really important.

Al's arms went around her, and she lifted up on tip-toe. His lips found hers, and all those perfectly-working parts began to hum. The tinglies she had felt before intensified.

Just before she stopped thinking altogether, Bubbles made her choice.

What the hell. There were always other jobs.

* * *

Al watched from the rail, as his wife—his wife!—prepared for the between-races entertainment. We was proud of her, proud that she had found something she could excel at, even if it wasn't unicorn racing.

At least she was still working at the track.

In the infield, Bubbles adjusted the harness, and settled herself in the saddle. She waved at Al, a little shiver of pleasure passing through her, as she recalled the previous night. And anticipated the night to come.

This wasn't exactly unicorn racing, but it was still a respectable job.

She smiled at Al. He had been right, and so had Rainbow and Sunshine, who stood with him at the rail.

She braced herself, as the cow's muscles bunched beneath her. The cat raised his fiddle, and Bubbles took a deep breath.

"To the moon!" she whispered.

Cheer Witches

Cheer Witches

THE MUSIC WAS LOUD, loud enough to cover Cassie's voice as she counted the beat. She linked arms with Lynn on the third level of the human pyramid, and waited, a huge smile locked in place.

Behind her, unseen, and unheard beneath the pounding beat, Cassie knew Allison was starting her run.

Four beats, and Allison jumped into the waiting hands.

Two beats, she landed on Cassie's and Lynn's shoulders.

One beat to catch her balance.

One beat to raise her arms in a giant "V" for victory.

"Go, Salem!" Cassie screamed in unison with the rest of the squad.

They had rehearsed the routine a thousand times, maybe several thousand, but each time Cassie held her breath as Allison's foot landed on her shoulder, as her toes, in their soft slipper, dug in and Allison stood atop the pyramid. Each time Cassie knew they teetered twenty feet in the air, a split second from disaster; from broken bones and career-ending injuries.

Allison's foot slid, as it had before, and Cassie felt her struggle to keep her balance. In that instant, she knew it was too late. Allison was falling.

Then, as though pushed by an invisible hand, Allison straightened and stood tall, and the squad below moved into position for the dismount.

Seconds later, Allison dived gracefully from her perch, her brush with disaster apparently forgotten.

On the gym floor, two strong boys caught her, breaking her fall and tossing her lightly onto her feet, where she slid into a split, her arms high in the air.

Lynn followed, then Cassie, as the pyramid came apart with practiced precision.

In the locker room after practice, Cassie lingered in the showers. When she emerged, wrapped in the scratchy gym towel, her hair dripping down her back, she found Allison alone in the locker bay. She was already dressed, with her letter sweater thrown carelessly over her shoulders.

"Allison."

Allison turned to look at Cassie. Her expression wasn't unfriendly, just dismissive, as though Cassie wasn't worth the effort to dislike. "What?" she asked, making no effort to disguise her impatience.

"You know what. You nearly fell. And it isn't the first time." Cassie felt her face growing hot.

She didn't want this confrontation, shouldn't have to do it. But if Coach Barkley wasn't going to call Cassie on her missed landing—which was totally his responsibility—somebody had to. She couldn't be the only one who had noticed, could she?

"I didn't 'nearly fall,'" Allison said. "I landed just fine. Maybe my foot slipped a little, but it wouldn't have, if you weren't sliding all over the place."

A hot flash of anger raced through Cassie. She had not been sliding around! She had been steady and solid, and Allison knew it.

"That is such a lie!"

"Oh, yeah? Well, who do you think Coach will believe? His top, or," she waved a dismissive hand at Cassie, "the jealous little girl who had to settle for second place?"

Allison tried to look unconcerned, but Cassie sensed a moment of hesitation. Allison knew she was right.

"This isn't about me. Or you, Allison. It's about the team, and winning, and not getting my friends hurt because you won't admit you can't cut it."

Cassie turned away in disgust, yanking clothes from her locker. She wrestled a T-shirt over her head, and tried to ignore the tightness in her throat and the stinging in her eyes.

She would not let that bitch make her cry!

"Don't kid yourself, Cassie. I can cut it. I did it today, and I'll do it tomorrow, and I'll do it at the competition next week. And all your saying otherwise won't make it so."

Allison's locker slammed shut, the clash of metal echoing through the empty building. Cassie heard her stomp away, keeping her back turned until she was sure Allison was gone.

Was she really just jealous? Sure, Allison was the top. She was the smallest, lightest girl on the squad—the easiest for the guys to toss high into the air. Her long blond ponytail fanned out just-so when she tumbled, and her dad had paid a fortune for her dazzling smile.

There was a lot to be jealous of, but that wasn't it.

Allison had stumbled. She had nearly fallen, and Cassie knew it. Allison knew it, too. Cassie had seen it.

So what had saved her? It couldn't be witchcraft; that was strictly forbidden in competition. Get caught using a spell, or a wand, and you were off the squad, and getting cut was like total social suicide. Even Allison couldn't get away with that one.

Still, she was right about one thing. Nobody was going to believe Cassie, not without something to back up her suspicions.

So, what was she going to do about it?

* * *

Alone in her backyard, Cassie bounced on the trampoline her parents had installed for her to train on. It was supposed to help her practice, to make her the best, but that plan hadn't quite worked.

Cassie bounced on her butt, then back onto her feet, and turned a somersault in mid-air. She didn't need to be jealous of Allison, she could have everything Allison had, if she wanted it badly enough. All she needed was to starve herself, use lots of bleach, and spend a fortune on dentist bills—and she didn't want it that bad.

The tramp rolled under her feet with the weight of another body, dropping her onto her back.

Cassie looked up at Dave, the cheerleader-next-door, and her best friend since second grade. Dave grinned and held out his hand, hauling her back onto her feet.

They bounced in companionable silence for a minute, then Cassie said "Dave?"

"That's me."

"Can I ask you something?"

Dave furrowed his brow. "Of course. Isn't that what friends are for?"

"Yeah." She paused a second before the words rushed out. "Am I a jealous bitch?"

"Did I say you were?"

"No. But someone else did."

Dave put his hands on her shoulders, forcing her to stop bouncing. He gave her a little shove toward the side of the tramp and sat down, patting the rubber next to him.

"And the person was—hmm, let me guess—Allison?"

Cassie dropped down next to him. "Well, duh! Guess that was pretty obvious, huh?"

"Yep." Dave smiled at her. "You don't have anything to be jealous about, anyway. Your spells are better, your grades are higher. If anything, she should be jealous of you."

Cassie thought for a minute before she spoke. "But Allison thinks I want her spot. Not that I wouldn't like it," she added quickly.

"Hello? I know all this already. Tell me something new."

"Well," Cassie drew the one word out, until it was nearly a whole sentence. "See, I kinda think, that is, I know, that Allison, well, it's like." Cassie shook her head, annoyed at herself for stalling.

"Allison almost fell." There, she'd said it out loud.

"When?"

"Today, on the final pyramid. I felt her slip, and I thought we were all going down, but she pulled it out. And it wasn't the first time, either. She's come close to falling a lot of times, but she never does."

Dave hopped to his feet. Now it was his turn to think, to avoid looking at Cassie. He turned several flips while Cassie bounced at his side, waiting for him to say something, anything.

"You think she's cheating." It wasn't a question.

"I don't know what I think," Cassie said. "I mean, her spells aren't that good—you're right—she'd totally give herself away. And Coach won't even allow a wand into the gym, so there's no way…" Her voice trailed off.

"Then how—?" Dave began.

"I don't know," Cassie cut him off, feeling foolish. "I'm just saying, if she is, and we get caught, there goes the season. And probably next year, too."

She bounced higher, turning a somersault. "You'd tell me if I was being a bitch, wouldn't you?"

Dave grinned at her. "How could I pass up the opportunity?" Then he stopped smiling, and his voice lowered. "No, you're not. Really. I saw it, too." He shook his head. "I didn't want to believe it, told myself I was imagining things, she was too far away for me to be sure. But, I knew."

Cassie threw her arms around Dave's neck. "Thank you. I knew it wasn't just me!"

"No, not just you," Dave said. He plopped back down onto the trampoline, and rested his head on one fist. "But how do we get anybody to believe us? Like you said, Allison will just say you're jealous."

Cassie sat down beside him, and stared into the growing darkness. "Whatever we do, it better be fast. The finals in Worchester are in five days. After that, we're toast."

* * *

The next afternoon, Cassie dragged herself to the gym. She didn't know what to expect from Allison, and she dreaded another confrontation.

In the locker room, Allison was holding court, going out of her way to compliment the other squad members on their outfits.

Two days earlier, Cassie had heard her making barking noises to her friends when Cindy Martin walked past. Now, she was offering her makeup tips, and patting her shoulder like they were old friends.

Cassie spun the dial on her lock, glancing in Allison's direction. Allison avoided her glance, until she though no one else was looking, then glared. The message was as clear as if she had shouted "Don't screw with me!", and Cassie knew she had been warned.

This was war, and Allison was quickly gathering her allies.

Despite Cassie's fears, the practice seemed to go well. Each movement was precise, the timing was flawless, and Allison landed the final pyramid solidly.

When she finally followed Lynn, diving into the waiting arms of Dave and Robert, Cassie knew they had a winning routine.

If they could do this every time. But could they?

She hurried through her shower, trying to time her exit to avoid Allison, yet still be part of the noisy crowd spilling out of the locker room.

As she stepped outside, she could see Allison a few feet away. Cassie slowed her steps, putting more distance between them. Then Allison climbed into Brad's red Miata, and was gone.

Cassie considered her options. As though she had any. She could try to talk to Coach Barkley, but after their perfect practice, why would he have any reason to believe her?

Still, she had to try.

But when she poked her head in the coach's office, the only person there was the team manager, Franklin Pearson. He was writing awkwardly with his left hand on equipment forms. The long sleeves of his sweatshirt were pulled down, nearly covering his right hand.

"Uh, hi, Franklin." Nobody ever called him by anything but Franklin. "Coach's gone, huh?"

"Right after practice. Left me in charge." Franklin puffed his chest out, stressing his importance. "I was just finishing up. What can I do for you?"

"Oh, nothing. I just had a question for the coach, but it can wait."

"All right." Franklin sounded disappointed that he didn't get to be 'in charge' of some problem. "You're sure?"

"Sure," Cassie said. "Well, I better get going. Lots of homework."

Franklin shrugged. "If you say so." He stared at her for a second, and she was suddenly aware that they were alone in the building. "Sure you don't want to hang around? I'll be through here in just a minute."

"Naw, I gotta run," she said, stepping back from the door. "Later!"

As she hurried toward home, Cassie wondered why she had felt so uncomfortable around Franklin. He was team manager, but she didn't know him that well, since he had transferred to Witch High—oops, Salem Township Public High School #4—last fall.

She had heard rumors, though. He was a star tumbler at his last school, until an accident ended his career. His right arm, which he kept hidden, had been damaged. Some people said he'd lost it completely, but no one had ever actually seen it, and nobody really knew.

The one thing Cassie was sure of was that Franklin knew just about everything there was to know about cheering and about competitions. Even though he couldn't flip, or tumble, or do a cartwheel, he was still a part of the team.

And he wanted to win.

* * *

It took Cassie two more precious days to get an opportunity to talk to Coach Barkley. She changed her mind at least a half-dozen times, and she was still not sure what she was going to say when she finally walked into Coach's office and found him by himself.

"Can I talk to you, Coach?"

"Certainly, Cassie. Sit down." Coach gestured to the beat-up folding chair next to his desk. "What's the problem?"

Cassie closed the door behind her before she sat down. "I, uh, I don't know. That is, I do know, but I don't really know if it's a problem. It's just that, well," she swallowed hard, "I think there might be a problem, and I don't know what to do about it."

A flash of impatience crossed Coach's face, but he sat quietly, waiting for her to go on.

"It's Allison." There she'd said it. "She's missed a couple landings. One last week, and again this afternoon. She didn't fall, I know," she hurried on. "But I felt her slip. Really."

The coach's face hardened, and Cassie felt her stomach drop somewhere around her sneakers. Even before he opened his mouth, she knew he didn't believe her.

"Miss Stevens." Oh, shit. She'd gone from "Cassie" to "Miss Stevens." She'd be lucky if she wasn't cut from the team right here.

"That's a very serious accusation. Have you thought about what you're saying?" He held up his hand, and slowly unfolded his fingers as he talked.

His voice was soft, and serious. "First, Allison did not fall, despite what you say. In fact, she looked just fine from where I was. Second, if she did slip, and that's a very big 'if,' it was not apparent. Third, no one else saw or felt this slip. Fourth, there was no fault, no foul, no fall. Nothing that would mark down points in competition."

He stared at her, daring her to argue, and she knew she was defeated. He hadn't threatened to cut her—yet—but the hard look in his eyes was enough. She knew better than to say anything more, but she couldn't help herself.

"But, Coach," she said, trying to control the quaver in her voice. "It felt like she slipped, and then something just pushed her back into place."

Coach's eyes were hard and angry, and his face turned red. When he finally spoke, his voice cut through Cassie, sending a chill down her back. "Are you saying Allison was cheating somehow? That there was something else involved?

"You know how I feel about witchcraft in my gym, Miss Stevens. It is strictly forbidden. Spells and tricks are just lazy shortcuts that prevent you from actually learning our routines. None of my athletes would dare to break that rule."

Cassie knew she had already gone too far, and she struggled to keep from answering. Nothing she could say would make things better, and anything she could say would make things worse.

She nodded silently, and rose from her seat. Fighting for control, willing her eyes not to flood with tears of humiliation and rejection, she turned quickly and opened the door. The best thing she could do was leave, before coach threw her out of his office and off the squad.

Franklin was waiting next to the door, his face as hard and cold as the coach's. Had he been listening? Did he know what she had told Coach? Judging by his expression, the answer was yes.

She ran down the corridor, headed for the gym doors. Her chest was tight, and she needed to get outside, to get a breath of fresh air. She burst through the door, and didn't stop running until she reached her trampoline.

The familiar bouncing, up and down, soothed Cassie's frazzled nerves. As she calmed down, she wondered if what she had done was really as bad as she first thought.

She had spoken to the coach, and no one else. She hadn't gossiped with the other girls, or tried to confront Allison again. Coach Barkley was the only one who knew about her suspicions, and he had clearly dismissed them.

So why did she think he was wrong?

She was still trying to figure out how to get back on the coach's good side when Dave jumped up beside her.

"What's wrong?"

They had been friends a long time. Cassie knew she couldn't fool him. No sense in trying. "I talked to Coach after practice today. I told him Cassie slipped, and that it happened before."

"And—let me guess—he didn't believe you, right?" Dave shook his head. "What did you expect, Cassie? You knew he wouldn't believe it!"

"I know," she said miserably. "But I at least thought he'd listen. Instead, he said I was accusing Allison of cheating, and he didn't allow witchcraft on the squad, and nobody would break that rule."

She told him about nearly running into Franklin at the office door, and her suspicion that he'd been listening in.

"The worst part, though," she continued, "is that he's right. Not even Allison would break that rule. Nobody would. The squad is too important, we've worked too hard, to do anything that would hurt the team."

Cassie sat down, hanging her head and once more near tears. Maybe Allison wasn't her BFF, but she still wasn't a cheat, and Cassie hadn't really meant to imply she was.

"Then why did you say anything to Coach? You knew better!"

"But something's wrong, Dave! You said so yourself. Allison isn't sticking her landings, and she almost fell the other day." Cassie looked up at Dave. "You saw her today, too! I know you did."

She could see the answer in his eyes. He had seen Allison slip. He knew she was right.

Dave sat down next to her and nodded his head. "That still doesn't solve anything, though. Just because I think I saw something from the floor doesn't make it so. And if Coach didn't see it, it doesn't matter."

"Then what can we do about it? I want to win at semis—we all do—and if Allison doesn't make her landing, or if she's doing something that gets us disqualified, then we all lose!"

Dave patted Cassie's shoulder. "If Coach says it's okay, then it's okay. No matter what we think we saw. He wouldn't let anything hurt the squad's chances. You know that."

Cassie leaned her cheek against Dave's hand. "I know." She sighed, and dropped to the ground. "Guess I better go get my homework done. Thanks for being such a good listener, Dave."

Dave grinned at her and waved as he went through the high wooden gate between their back yards. Cassie waved back before the gate closed, and went in the house.

* * *

If Cassie had accepted what Dave said, and she had, there was only one thing she could do. Apologize. She needed to build a bridge and just get over herself, and the sooner the better.

As soon as the bell rang for lunch, she hurried across campus to Coach Barkley's office. When she got there, Coach was sitting behind his desk, and Franklin was in the other chair.

Coach greeted her politely, without a trace of his anger from the previous day, but Franklin glared at her, and didn't speak.

"Coach, can I talk to you for a minute?" Cassie asked. She didn't say "alone," but the coach got the idea anyway.

So did Franklin. He glared at Cassie, then turned to Coach Barkley as though looking for instructions. The coach nodded quickly at Franklin.

Franklin stood up and kicked the chair away, still glaring at Cassie. He brushed past her, not close enough to actually push her, but enough that she pulled back as he passed.

"Sit down, Cassie."

Well, at least she was "Cassie" again, and not "Miss Stevens." That was a good sign, wasn't it?

Still, she preferred to stay standing. Her breakfast felt like a lump in her stomach, and she twisted her fingers together to keep her hands from shaking. If she sat down, she might never be able to stand back up.

Cassie could dive from the top of the pyramid, do a double flip from a standing start, or walk a tightrope if she had to, all without a single nervous twitch or second of anxiety. But just thinking about this conversation had her weak in the knees.

She swallowed past the lump in her throat. "I came to apologize," she said. "I really though Allison had slipped, but I must be wrong. I shouldn't have said anything, and I apologize."

With the worst part out of the way, she took a deep breath and went on. "I didn't talk to anyone else about this. Except I tried to talk to Allison before I came to you, which didn't go so well, and I'll apologize to her as soon as I can. I just wanted to talk to you first."

Coach Barkley fiddled with a small glass paperweight from his desk. It was in the shape of a crystal ball. Cassie watched him turning the ball over in his hands, and wondered if he had powers, like the rest of the faculty.

She had never thought about it before. Witchcraft was strictly forbidden in the gym, but Coach could still practice outside the gym, right?

"Yes."

Cassie jumped, startled to have him answer her question out loud, even though she hadn't said a word.

"I don't allow anyone to use their power in here, usually not even me. It isn't fair to use our skills in competition with the mundane world, so they are banned from practice. If we rely on wands and spells, we don't gain the athletic skills we need to be competitive, and we don't learn sportsmanship and fair play."

"I never meant to say Allison was a cheat. She wants to win as much as the rest of us, but she wouldn't cheat. We may not be best friends," Cassie shrugged, "but she isn't a cheat."

"I know that," Coach answered, looking at the glass ball in his hand. "I wouldn't tolerate a cheat on my squad. And believe me," he said, gently laying the ball on his desk, "I know my squad."

"Understood, sir," Cassie said. Now that she had said what she needed to, she wanted to get out of there. Fast. Before her shaky knees stopped working entirely.

"I better hurry, if I want to talk to Allison before lunch is over," she said as she opened the door. "Thanks, Coach."

"Thank you, Cassie. See you at practice."

Cassie darted out the door and turned toward the cafeteria, only to find her way blocked by Franklin.

"Haven't you done enough?" he said, his voice low. "Just leave Allison alone. She doesn't need any more of your interference; she's fine just the way she is."

"What I do is none of your business, Franklin. That was a private conversation."

"I'm the team manager." He stood tall, and looked down at her. "Coach expects me to keep track of everything, so it is my business. I have to take care of the squad at all times."

Cassie stared into Franklin's cold eyes. "I'm not so sure Coach Barkley," she raised her voice a little, wondering if the coach could overhear the conversation outside his door, "would appreciate you eavesdropping when he's got the door closed."

"I need to know what's going on."

There was no point in arguing with Franklin, and Cassie had to go find Allison. She wanted this over with.

"Whatever!" she said, stepping around Franklin.

As she walked away, she heard him go in Coach Barkley's office and close the door.

Creepazoid, much?

She shook her head, and hurried on toward the cafeteria.

For once, Allison wasn't the center of an adoring crowd in the cafeteria, and Cassie was able to slide onto an empty bench across from her. She glanced at Allison's plate, where a squashed lemon wedge and a few droopy lettuce leaves were considered a meal. Yuck!

"What do you want?" Allison said, as soon as she sat down. She wasn't pleased to see Cassie, especially without her audience of adoring fans, but this time Allison's mood wouldn't control Cassie.

"I came to apologize," she said. She kept her voice low and soft, trying to feel some sympathy for the girl across the table. After all, she carried a lot of responsibility on her thin shoulders, and Cassie had added to that this week.

"I am really sorry. I did think you slipped, and I was worried about the semis. We all want to win, and I was afraid. But if you say you didn't slip, well, maybe I was nervous or something, and I was wrong."

Cassie bit her lip, and looked at Allison. There was something—fear?—deep in Allison's eyes, but it disappeared before Cassie could be sure.

Allison shrugged, and a smile curved her mouth, though it didn't change the blank look in her eyes. "Apology accepted."

Cassie blew out a deep breath. "Thanks, Allison. I just wanted to get this out of the way. I mean, we have semis in just a couple days, and I know we can win."

Allison nodded. "Yes, we can." But there was a hesitation in her voice.

Or maybe Cassie was just imagining things again. After all, Allison had done the same routine about a million times, and she was perfect almost every time.

There was nothing to worry about.

* * *

The music was loud, loud enough to cover Cassie's voice as she counted the beat. She linked arms with Lynn on the third level of the human pyramid, and waited, a huge smile locked in place.

Behind her, unseen, and unheard beneath the pounding beat, Cassie knew Allison was starting her run. In front of her, the audience in the Worchester Arena was a sea of faces, all run together. They clapped in time to the music, adding to the noise and the insistent rhythm.

Beat, beat, beat, beat. Lift. Beat, beat. Land.

Allison's weight, all eighty-seven pounds of her, was steady on Cassie's shoulder, a perfect landing. She felt Allison shift slightly, as she threw her arms in the air, still solid and steady.

Beat.

"Go, Salem!"

The crowd exploded in cheers and applause, shrill whistles echoing from the left side. Cassie's dad was sitting there, and even though she couldn't see him, she knew he had his fingers in the corner of his mouth, whistling wildly.

Relief was a warm tide, flowing through Cassie's body. They were perfect! The only thing left was the dismount. The crowd loved them! And if the crowd loved, them, the judges would love them, too!

Allison tensed, shifting slightly as she braced herself, then dove for the floor. Cassie held her head high, eyes forward, but she heard another explosion of applause, and she knew Allison had landed in a perfect split in front of the pyramid.

Beside her, Lynn launched herself, and a few beats later Cassie dove into the waiting arms of the catchers.

But Dave wasn't there.

Charlie and Wade caught her, and swung her onto her feet. She tried to look around, to spot Dave without breaking the routine, but she couldn't find him.

There was no time for distractions. Cassie made her last move, a stag leap into Charlie's arms, and held her position, as the crowd cheered and stomped.

A whistle blew, from the edge of the stage, a signal for the squad to break formation and make their exit.

As Cassie moved toward the wings, her heart turned a flip, higher and wilder than any the squad had performed in the last four minutes.

Franklin was on the floor, his shirt ripped away. Dave knelt with one knee on his chest, his uniform torn, and a trickle of blood on the side of his face. Franklin was twisting awkwardly on the ground, trying to get away.

A judge was standing over the two boys, his hands in fists on his hips, and a security guard was reaching for something clutched in Dave's hand.

Her stomach lurched at the sight of the blood on Dave's face. She raced to the spot where the boys still struggled, as the security guard tried to intervene. Coach Barkley was only a step or two in front of her.

She was within a step or two when her brain finally registered what Dave was holding. She stopped dead, staring, as the realization hit her.

Franklin's right shoulder was bare, a horrifying mass of scar tissue and strap marks, where his prosthetic arm had been ripped away. And Dave had hold of an arm.

A wooden arm.

An arm that could double as a wand.

Dave caught her eye. His head moved slightly, a little shake that no one else noticed.

The security guard pulled Dave off Franklin, and helped the manager to his feet. Dave surrendered the arm to Coach Barkley, refusing to return it to Franklin.

Coach's eyes widened as he realized what he was holding, but Dave said quietly, "It's okay, Coach."

"We'll sort this out in the office." The security guard gestured for the group to follow him down a hallway.

Cassie ran to Dave before the guard could lead them away, and threw her arms around his neck.

"You said—" she whispered in Dave's ear.

"I know. But you were so sure. And you were right," Dave interrupted. "I was watching, and I stopped him before he could interfere. Allison did it by herself."

The guard pulled her away, and Cassie reached up to brush the blood away from Dave's temple.

"It'll be okay," Dave assured her, as he walked down the hall, Coach Barkley at his side. "I'll tell you all about it later."

The cheers of the audience still rang in her ears. They'd earned it fairly and honestly. For today, they were perfect.

Loves Me Knot

Loves Me Knot

FRANKLIN PHILLIPS COULDN'T REMEMBER a time in his nearly seventy years when he didn't love Emily Gordon. She was wealthy, beautiful, and smart. Well, mostly smart—except for her abysmal taste in men.

In that, she was incredibly, blindly stupid.

Despite his devotion, she had barely spoken to Franklin in more than fifty years.

It all started with the roses.

No, scratch that. It ended with the roses. It started the first time Franklin laid eyes on her.

First grade. Mrs. Miles class. The smell of chalk dust tickled Franklin's nose when we walked in at the end of a line of boys, all arranged by height. Rows of desks lined the room, their hinged wood tops scarred from their ongoing battles with six-year-olds.

He hung his stiff cotton jacket with the elbow patches on a hook, and put his shiny metal lunch box on the shelf above, as Mrs. Miles told them to do, then turned around to find the desk with his name on it.

That was when he saw Emily Gordon for the first time. Sitting primly in the desk next to his, her hands folded on the desktop, tidy dark braids hanging down her back. She smiled at him as he slid into his seat, her dark eyes shining with a hidden mischief that was at odds with her proper exterior.

From that twinkle, and that smile, he was a goner. Although, being a six-year-old boy, he didn't know why.

They were friends from the first; playing together after school, and helping each other with homework. Franklin was a natural athlete, and he taught Emily to swim that first summer, cheering her on from the side of her family's Olympic-size pool. Her smile the first time she managed an entire lap of the pool was a reward worth more than his entire robot collection. Well, except for that one Gundai with the cool sword.

Emily had a sword, too. At least, her family did. He saw it one day when he was playing at her house.

It was very old. Older than anything he had ever seen, except in the museum on their second-grade field trip. It was in a big glass case in the room Emily called the library; a dark-paneled room with soft leather chairs that creaked when you sat in them.

Franklin stared at the glass case, squinting at the scratches along the short blade. Emily came up beside him, pointing to a card inside the case. "My dad says this belonged to some guy named Alex." She shrugged. "It's really old."

Franklin didn't want to admit that he couldn't read the elegant cursive script on the card, so he just nodded his head. Besides, the sword was kind of small, and beat up looking, not like the Gundai's shiny plastic sword. He matched Emily's shrug, and the two of them ran off to the garden to play hide-and-seek, the sword forgotten.

The gardens were a magical place for small children to play. The carefully trimmed hedges and the twisting paths provided hiding places, while the air was filled with the scent of flowers in every season.

Spring, Emily told him, was her favorite season, when the roses started blooming. She loved the roses, from the miniatures in pale hues of yellow and pink, to the extravagant blood-red blossoms of the hybrids, to the rich perfume of the climbing roses that covered the small pergola in the middle of the garden. The pergola was her favorite place to hide, and Franklin always checked there first when he was "it."

The pergola was where he kissed her the first time; before things went bad. So maybe it started with the roses, too.

They were thirteen, a little old for hide-and-seek; unwilling to relinquish the closeness of their childhood friendship, yet finding a new awareness of each other, and an attraction that was exciting, and frightening and oh, so wonderful, all at the same time.

It was dusk in early summer. A time when the air still held the warmth of the day, but a promise of a cool evening to come. The sun had set, and the shadows ran together into a soft, gray blanket that was more dream than reality.

Franklin knew he would have to go home soon. His mother would expect him for dinner, and lately she had seemed less pleased at the amount of time he spent with Emily. Still, he wanted to delay his departure as long as he could.

He knew Emily was hiding in the pergola, knew he could find her at any time. But it would end the game, and the day.

Instead, he wandered the garden paths, deliberately crunching the gravel so as to give away his location. He circled the pergola several times, occasionally pausing as though he was about to step inside and discover her.

He could imagine her waiting, surrounded by banks of fragrant climbing roses, the air heavy with their scent. She would be close to the flowers, letting the silky petals brush against her cheek, so that she would carry their fragrance for hours afterward. Sometimes, when he caught her unaware, she would have her eyes closed, as if concentrating on the rich, sweet smell.

He walked a few feet along the path, following a rose hedge toward the pool, then doubled back. He placed his sneakered feet carefully, so that he made no sound.

Twilight had deepened, and soon the garden lights, triggered by the coming dark, would switch on, and the dreamy dusk would be chased away.

He took two more stealthy steps, and he was inside the pergola. The twisted vines and thick foliage blocked the remaining light. Under the canopy of roses, it was as black as night, and he could hear Emily breathing shallowly in the dark.

His lips parted, her name forming in his mind before reaching his mouth. He knew her reaction, the muffled giggle, and sigh of surrender that would signal the end of the game.

But he didn't want it to end that way. Not today. Today there was some kind of magic in the air that made him stop before he spoke. Instead he paused to listen, to locate Emily by the sound of her breathing, to move closer to her.

He was close enough to feel the faint warmth of the sun radiating off her bare arm. To smell the sweet peppermint of her chewing gum. And he knew, by the way she stiffened and held very still, that she knew he was there.

There was no time to think, or plan, or consider the consequences. He leaned toward the smell of peppermint, toward the sound of her soft breathing, and kissed her.

It was over almost as soon as it started. Both of them drew back in surprise. Franklin's heart was racing so fast he thought it might break right out of his chest and run away.

"Hi," Emily said, very softly. "You found me."

"Yeah." Franklin drew back, unsure of what to do next. Should he try to kiss her again? Ask her if he could? Ask if she liked it? It had seemed like an okay kiss to him, but he had to admit, he didn't really have anything to compare it to.

But before he could decide, the garden lights flickered on, sending shadows dancing through the vines, and driving away the magical darkness that had made him bold.

"I, uh, I better go," he said, jamming his hands in the pockets of his jeans. "Mom expects me home for dinner."

"Okay," Emily said, her voice soft. "See you tomorrow."

Franklin wondered if this meant Emily was becoming his girlfriend. He had never thought about having a girlfriend, even though some of the guys at school did. He didn't know if he wanted a girlfriend. But he liked Emily, and he had kissed her, after all.

Maybe she was his girlfriend.

Franklin never thought of Emily as his rich girlfriend, even though he knew other people sometimes did. Besides, he wasn't exactly poor. Maybe his house wasn't quite as big, and he didn't have museum-old swords and paintings, or fancy rose gardens, but it was still pretty nice. His dad's landscaping business provided what his mother called "a comfortable living."

Comfortable enough that when Franklin turned sixteen, they bought him a car for his birthday. But the car came with a very large string attached, in the form of a summer job to pay for his insurance.

He tried to argue, but his dad wasn't buying it.

"Last I knew, cars don't grow on trees, and neither does insurance money." His dad chuckled. "If they did, my clients wouldn't want anything else in their yards."

Franklin rolled his eyes. That was supposed to be "landscape humor," but he didn't think it was funny for his dad to be laughing about ruining his summer.

"But I have to train for the swim team, and I have two afternoons a week at the library with the biology study project. I don't have time to spend in the office, helping you design projects."

"Excuse me?" His dad sounded annoyed. "First, I need an employee, and you need the insurance money if you want to drive that car. Second, you can work mornings and keep up your afternoon activities.

"And, third, who said you'd be in the office?"

"Well, isn't that what I usually do for you? Help with the designs?"

"Frank," dad was now using his patient voice, a sure sign of trouble. "You watch me design, and yes, you have a very good eye. You make some good suggestions. But I need someone on the crew; someone to prune and mow and plant. Which, by the way, will help build up your arms and shoulders for swimming."

Franklin looked at his mom, hoping for help, but he knew from her expression that she had already talked to his dad, and they had agreed that Franklin was working on the crew for the summer. No sense even talking about it.

Still, it might not be all bad.

After having Emily as his girlfriend for nearly three years, maybe it was time to take the next step. He was only sixteen, but he knew that he loved her, that he had always loved her. If he was working, maybe he could save a little money, and buy her the promise ring he'd been considering. Sure, they were young, too young some people would say, but he knew she was the only woman in the world for him.

Besides, it wasn't like they were getting engaged or anything. It was just a promise that he would always love her.

That was a promise he could keep forever.

Franklin's dad kept him busy every morning, and most afternoons, when he wasn't at the library. He missed the time with Emily, though she was busy, too. Still, the guys on the crews were nice to him, and the growing balance in his bank account would more than pay for the ring he wanted.

He noticed, though, that his dad kept him off the crew that worked on the Gordons' gardens. He didn't think it was a coincidence. He knew every inch of that garden, he had played there with Emily for ten years or more, yet he was never on that crew.

He wanted to be on the crew. It would be great to be able to see Emily in the morning, when he got to work. Sure, he couldn't talk to her while he was working, but he could see her.

And she would be able to see him, see the new muscles that were growing in his arms and chest and shoulders. Sometimes they would work with their shirts off, and he could imagine her watching him, seeing how strong he had become.

He wished he could get the chance to show off for her, but oh, so casually, just doing his job in the heat of the day.

A wise man once said to be careful what you wish for. But Franklin wasn't a wise man. He was a sixteen-year-old boy, crazy in love, and wanting desperately to impress the girl he loved. He would have a very long time to regret that particular wish.

Clayton, the third man on the Gordon crew, called in sick on a Thursday morning. It wouldn't have been a problem, they could have simply caught up the work the next week, except the Gordons were having important guests, and the gardens had to be perfect. Franklin took Clayton's place.

He was going to work at Emily's! His wish was coming true, and he couldn't wait to see the look on Emily's face when he casually took off his shirt, and flexed his muscles.

It was several hours, nearly the end of his day's work, before he actually saw her. She came out of the house, headed toward the pool, her swimsuit covered by a filmy coat that didn't hide her curves.

His chest tightened when he saw her. His shirt was off, and he drew in a deep breath, pulling in his already-flat stomach, and puffing up his chest.

But when she saw him, her look wasn't admiration for his physique. She wasn't impressed by his bulging arms, or broad shoulders. She looked almost sad to see him there.

Rattled, unable to understand the expression of hurt on Emily's face, Franklin tried to continue his work, to show her what he could do.

But his hands and arms wouldn't follow the directions from his brain. They seemed to want to go everywhere but where he wanted them to, swinging his clippers in the wrong direction.

His hand slipped. He saw one blade bump into the corner post of the pergola, threatening to nick the brilliant white paint, and just managed to turn the handles to avoid damaging the structure's pristine finish.

He grabbed for the handles with his other hand, gaining an awkward grip on the second handle. He knew he looked like a total klutz, and he knew Emily was watching, but he was more concerned with not hurting anything, including himself, with the sharp blades.

He gripped the handles, meshing the blades together, hearing them slide against each other in a smooth, slick whisper.

The blades stuck for a split second, but before he could react, they moved again, their finely-honed edges slicing easily through several trailing vines of the antique roses that covered the pergola.

The severed vines dropped to the ground, leaving a gap in the curtain of roses that covered the end of the pergola. The jagged ends looked like a child's jack-o'-lantern, its jagged teeth widely spaced in its mouth.

Charlie, the crew chief, ran over. "What the hell was that?" he yelled, his face close to Franklin's.

"I, I slipped," said Franklin miserably.

Charlie followed Franklin's gaze, catching sight of Emily, her face contorted with anger. He looked back at Franklin, a knowing grin on his face.

"It's like that, is it?" He shook his head. "Seems like it's always about some woman.

"Here," he took the clippers from Franklin, set them on the ground, and pulled a small pair of pruners from his work belt. "Let me see what I can do. In the meantime, you go give Joe a hand with the grass trimmings."

Franklin nodded, too dejected to speak, and shuffled across the path to where Joe was dumping debris into the garden trailer.

Emily had disappeared, but not before Franklin had seen shock and anger replace the hurt in her expression.

The pergola had been their special place, and he had damaged it. He hoped she would forgive him.

But sixteen-year-old girls are as unforgiving as sixteen-year-old boys are clumsy. He spent the next four days trying to talk to her. She wouldn't take his calls, or come to the door when he knocked.

Finally, he followed her when she went shopping, and caught up with her in the parking lot of the coffee shop. Although he tried to explain, apologize, she refused to believe him.

"You were looking right at me," she screamed. "Right at me! It was like you were telling me we didn't matter, you could just cut me out of your life!"

"It wasn't like that." Franklin reached for her hand, the hand he had wanted to put a ring on, but she snatched it away. "You looked upset, like you had never seen me before, and you didn't like what you saw."

"It was just, I didn't expect to see you." She was crying now, tears running down her face. "I didn't even know it was you. I thought it was one of the gardeners."

Her words hit Franklin like a fist in his gut. She didn't love him because he was a gardener? He was a lot more than that, and she knew it!

"Is that what this is all about?" he shouted. Anger welled in his chest, and he felt like a balloon about to burst. If he did, he would cover her with his hot anger, burn her, hurt her.

And, angry as he was, he still didn't want to hurt her.

He clenched his fists, and stuffed them in his pockets, drawing all the anger into his hands, deflating the balloon in his chest.

"No. Yes. I don't know."

Emily couldn't give him an answer, not one he could understand. And he needed to understand, needed to know why she was treating him this way.

"You don't know?" His voice had dropped to a whisper. There was no way to make this better. If she didn't know how she felt, then he didn't belong here.

Emily shook her head, tears scattering from her chin onto the front of her shirt. Franklin wanted to reach out and wipe the tears away, to comfort her and stop her crying, but he couldn't. Not now.

He turned away, back toward his car.

He stopped after a couple steps, and looked back.

She was standing by her car door, keys still in her hand, tears still dropping off her chin.

"Call me when you do know," he said, a tinge of bitterness in his tone.

He jumped in the car and slammed the door, squealing the tires as he sped away.

Emily went away for her senior year of high school, much to Franklin's relief. It was awkward, seeing her in the halls at schools, or sitting in the same class with her, and not speaking. With her gone, he could pretend that his life was back to normal.

He could hope that when she came home, they could make up, and start over.

But Emily didn't come home. Instead, she chose to go to college in another state, while Franklin stayed closer to home.

He supposed he could have gone anywhere he wanted, but he wanted to be close, in case Emily decided to come home. He even added a class in romantic poetry, hoping he could learn the words he needed to win her back.

When the dinner invitation arrived, Franklin was delighted. Emily would be home, and her parents wanted him to come her first night back.

He practiced the things he would say to her, the things he would tell her. Maybe he could even get her to walk in the garden, to talk in the pergola, the place that had always been special to both of them.

But instead of a quiet reunion, Franklin found himself in a crowd of friends and family. Instead of a chance to plead his case, he barely got a chance to talk to Emily alone.

At last, she approached him, gesturing him to follow her into the library.

The room was just as he remembered. A fire flickered in the fireplace, sending shadows dancing across the dark wood paneling.

Emily sat in one of the leather chairs. He lowered himself into a chair next to her, the leather creaking quietly as he sat.

He could smell warm leather and wood polish, and a hint of rose, as if Emily had spent the afternoon in the pergola, soaking up the scent of the roses. But it was October, and there were no roses in bloom. Still, she smelled like roses.

"It's been a long time," he said.

"Too long, I'm afraid," Emily replied softly. "I should have talked to you before now."

"I would have liked that." He wanted to touch her, but she held herself aloof, making the distance between them feel like miles, rather than inches.

"I was just a kid." She said it as if that explained everything.

"We both were."

"My father still thinks I'm a child," she continued. "But he's wrong. I'm twenty years old, a grown woman. I'm old enough to know what I want."

Franklin felt his stomach clench. He knew, before she said the words, that what she wanted wasn't him.

"I'm going to be engaged. Tonight. That was the reason for the party." She sighed, and looked away. "I wanted to tell you first. I don't know why, really, but I didn't want you to hear it from someone else."

Franklin never remembered how he escaped from that room, from the soft clutch of the leather chair, the oppressive heat of the fire, the overwhelming odor of dying roses.

He didn't remember anything about the rest of the night. Just the pain that settled in his heart, and stayed.

Emily was married the next summer, but he declined the invitation to the wedding. He saw her picture in the newspaper, smiling on her father's arm, a bouquet of roses in her arms.

It wasn't the last wedding picture he saw. Over the years, Emily married three more times. Each time, Franklin read the announcement in the papers, and silently wished her well.

Each time, it ended in disaster—physical, emotional, or financial. Sometimes, all three. She had buried the last one only a few months before, and come back to her family home to live.

Now, she was only a few streets away.

Now, though they hadn't exchanged more than a dozen words in decades, he felt himself being pulled toward her house, the house and garden where he had fallen in love with her.

The house with the roses that had started it all. And ended it all.

Now, he wanted, needed, to talk to Emily. To put the memories to rest. And maybe, just maybe, to be friends again, before it was too late.

It was dusk. The early summer air was still warm with the day's sun, but it held a promise of a cool evening. Franklin wore a light jacket to ward off the chill that would settle in his joints.

But was it the weather, or the welcome that worried him more?

He approached the house, pausing at the sidewalk, overcome with the memories of childhood summer evenings, playing in the soft shadows.

He walked slowly up the curving driveway, watching the front door, as though he expected Emily, the Emily with dark braids and a twinkle of mischief in her eyes, to burst out and run down the drive toward him, yelling "You're It."

But the door stayed steadfastly closed, and Franklin realized all the windows were dark across the front of the house.

The irony was not lost on Franklin. Was it possible she wasn't even home?

He had avoided Emily for decades, until it became a habit. Now he was breaking that habit, inviting the pain and rejection back into his life. What if she was out shopping, or at her bridge club, or just seeing a movie? Worse, what if she was home, but she wasn't alone?

This was insane.

Yet he didn't stop. Something drove him forward, ignoring the warnings in his brain.

And when no one answered the door, even though he could hear the chimes echoing through the house, he didn't leave.

He needed to see the garden.

He followed the gravel path around the house, stepping as quietly as he could. He wasn't quite as nimble as the last time he walked this path, that last night he had seen her, but he moved quickly.

Something was wrong. Franklin sensed it as soon as he saw the garden. It was as neat and well-kept as it had always been, thanks to Phillips Landscape. His foreman saw to the Gordon estate personally.

Flowers bloomed along the path, pansies and impatiens, and marigolds in the riotous mix of colors that Emily had always loved, their display muted in the dusk. The garden lights hadn't yet come on.

The roses were carefully pruned, the hybrids lifting enormous blossoms on graceful vines, the miniatures creating patterns of yellow and pink and lavender in their small beds.

The heat of the day lingered, drawing the scent of the roses, and mixing it with the rich musk of freshly-turned mulch and fertilizer. Franklin realized with a start that his crew had been there earlier in the day.

As he reached the center of the garden, he glanced at the pergola. It was covered, as always, with a blanket of antique roses, their sweet fragrance carried to him on the faint breeze. But it didn't look right, somehow.

Well, he hadn't seen in it decades. Things change. Maybe it wasn't even the same pergola. Still, he would have known of any major changes in the garden. It would have been in the work orders that he reviewed every week.

No, something was definitely wrong.

He stopped and listened for a moment. The crunch of his footsteps in the gravel echoed in the silence. There was a faint sound, almost a whisper, coming from the pergola.

He stepped closer, the gravel crunching loudly under his shoes, then stopped again. Waiting.

He heard a deep breath, and then a soft voice.

"Who's there?"

It was her.

"It's Franklin. Franklin Phillips." He wondered if she would even remember him. "From the landscape company."

A sob came from the pergola, followed by a chuckle that flooded him with memory.

"I know who you are, Franklin!" There was a touch of amusement in her voice now, but he could still hear fear and uncertainty. "I, uh, well …"

She hesitated, and he took another step, peering through the gloom, trying to see under the pergola, but his view was blocked by a tangle of blossoms and vines.

"Franklin," she sounded less afraid, now that she knew who it was. "I need your help."

"What can I do?" he said, without hesitation.

"Get me out of here!" The fear was gone from her voice now, replaced by frustration. "The vines are too thick, I can't get out!"

"What do you mean, you can't get out?" he said, moving close to the pergola, and inspecting the vines. "Didn't my crew trim these this afternoon?"

"Of course they did! And when I came out to sit for a while, everything was fine. But when I got ready to go in, there was a huge tangle, and I couldn't get through."

The pergola shook as she kicked at an upright. "I was about ready to knock the damned thing down when I heard you walk into the garden.

"Now, please, get me out!"

The garden lights flickered on, and Franklin got his first good look at the climbing roses. They had been trimmed—he could see the careful shaping of the plant.

But he couldn't see a single end. The rest of the vines were knotted together in a mass of flowers and thorns, as though someone had twisted them around themselves until the ends had disappeared inside the knot.

He reached for a vine, trying to untwist the tangle, but a thorn caught his hand, piercing his finger and drawing a drop of bright red blood. Instinctively, he put his finger in his mouth, the salty taste of his own blood on his tongue.

"I'm gonna need some gloves," he said.

"In the kitchen. The closet next to the back door. There are some gardening things in there." The fear had returned. "Hurry!"

Franklin trotted up the walk, and opened the back door. He ignored the rush of memories, refused to think about the last time he had opened that door. He grabbed gloves from the closet, then took a moment to check out the other contents.

He might need some tools, and he quickly found a pair of clippers, lightweight ones designed for cutting flowers. He pawed through the closet, but couldn't find anything heavier. He stuck the clippers in the pocket of his jacket and ran back to the garden, pulling on the heavy leather gloves as he went.

"I'm back," he panted, as he reached the pergola. "Let me see what I can do."

With his hands protected by the heavy leather gloves, Franklin was able to grab the vines. He tugged at the knots, trying to work an end free, but they stubbornly refused to move.

"Franklin?"

"Yeah." He grunted with the effort of tugging at the knot.

"Why did you come here?"

"To the garden?" He yanked, but only succeeded in rattling the pergola. He heard leaves rattle to the ground inside. "Because no one answered the door."

"No. Why did you come to the house? You haven't, you know, in a very long time."

Franklin thought about it, as he struggled with the knot of vines. Words, the words he had thought he'd find in his poetry, failed him. He just had to do it.

"Franklin?"

"I don't know, Emily. I just had to come over."

He reached in his pocket, taking out the clippers.

He remembered the last time he had tried to trim these roses, the day that a clumsy sixteen-year-old boy had lost his true love.

Maybe this time he could do a better job.

But the clippers couldn't even cut through the vines. The handles twisted in his hand, and the blades slid impotently against the cruel thorns.

"Emily, this isn't working. I can't untangle this knot, and the clippers I found can't cut it." He let his arms fall to his sides.

"Then find something that will. I can't stay in here all night!"

"Right. Then I'll cut the rose vines, and we'll be back where we started, all those years ago!"

"What?!?"

"You know what. You dumped me over the roses. That first summer I worked for my dad. You dumped me because I was a gardener, and I botched up the roses."

"Franklin, for heaven's sake! I have no idea what you're talking about! You think I dumped you?" Her voice put quotes around the phrase, reminding Franklin of the mischief that had twinkled in her eyes. It made him smile, in spite of their growing argument.

"You did."

"My dad grounded me! I was failing math, and he made me go to summer school, and then he sent me away for senior year." She snorted. "Dumped you! You're the one that wouldn't talk to me after that day!

"Now get me out of here!"

"I'll be right back."

Franklin ran up the walk, through the door and back into the kitchen, his mind reeling with what Emily had said. Was it true? Had he misunderstood her, turned his back on her?

He rifled through the kitchen drawers, looking for a sturdy knife. He didn't want to, but he was going to have to cut his way through those vines, to get Emily out of the pergola.

But even the largest knife in the kitchen wasn't enough. He managed to saw through most of one vine, though it took several minutes. He pulled on the cut, trying to break loose an end, but the vine refused to break.

A tendril of panic wound around his chest. What if he couldn't get her out? He could go for help, but he didn't want to leave Emily alone.

"Emily? Are you okay?"

"I'm fine," she answered, but she didn't sound fine. She sounded tired, and angry.

He remembered that she didn't like being scared. Whenever she got scared, it made her mad.

Right now, she sounded very mad.

"Let me go see if I can find something else to cut these. Can you wait for me?"

"I've waited more than fifty years," she said. "I can wait a little longer."

Then, in a tone that he knew well, she continued. "But hurry up. I'm not getting any younger!"

Franklin was smiling as he ran back into the house. He didn't feel the fatigue that should have been dragging him down. He could do anything.

Franklin raced through the house, trying to find something, anything, that would cut through the knot.

He'd already checked the kitchen, and he passed through into the dining room. The sideboard was loaded with china and silver, but nothing useful.

In the hall, he turned toward the stairs. Maybe in the garage…

But there were no tools in the garage.

Back in the hall, he glanced around. Upstairs? Just bedrooms and bathrooms. Not likely to find anything there.

He was about to give up, when he another childhood memory tickled the back of his brain. If there was a fireplace in the library, maybe there was a small ax to chop kindling.

He stopped at the library door, and gritted his teeth. He had sworn he would never enter this door again. But Emily was counting on him. He swallowed hard, and swung the door open.

He could see the fireplace, see the heavy andirons and the log lifter. A broom and a small poker. A basket of logs, cut to fit the grate.

No ax.

Damn!

Something triggered another memory, and he turned to his left.

There it was.

The old sword.

Emily had said it belonged to someone named Alex. Not that it mattered much right now. All he needed was to cut the knot of rose vines, and free Emily from her rose-covered prison.

The sword still rested in its glass case, just as it had all those years ago. The card was still in the case, the spidery writing faded with the years, illegible in the dark room.

He wondered if the case had an alarm. No matter. If it did, then it would bring help.

He didn't see a latch, and didn't take a lot of time looking. He pulled his jacket over his face, and balled his fist inside the leather glove, then brought it down with all his strength on the top of the glass.

The sound of shattering glass was like a bomb in the quiet house.

He reached carefully though the hole, drew out the short blade, and ran from the house.

Franklin stood in front of the pergola, the sword gripped in his right hand. "Stand back," he ordered. "I'm going to try and cut this damned thing."

"What have you got?" she asked. He heard her move away from the entrance.

"That old sword."

She gasped. "But, that's—"

Franklin didn't wait for her to finish. He brought the sword down with all his might, wincing as the blade sliced cleanly through the knot of vines. In spite of everything, he hated to hurt the roses.

The pieces of the knot fell away, vines covering the ground with a carpet of roses, and Emily was in his arms.

"Thank you," she said, laying her head against his chest.

Franklin laughed. It felt so good to hold her.

He raised the sword into the air. "Any time. Maidens rescued, dragons slain.

"Sir Franklin Phillips, at your service."

"Well," she said, drawing back to look up at him, a smile lighting her face, and a touch of mischief once again shining in her eyes. "We had better get up to the house. The police will be here soon."

Franklin listened, hearing sirens in the distance, drawing closer with each passing second.

"An alarm?" he asked, though the answer seemed obvious.

She nodded.

"For a sword that belonged to 'Alex somebody'?"

She took his hand, and led him toward the house, as the siren screamed closer.

"I never really believed my father, but I was never sure. He claimed it belonged to Alexander the Great."

She glanced back over her shoulder.

"Considering what it did to that knot, maybe he was right."

The Case of the Tale Spinner

The Case of the Tale Spinner

THE SMELL OF MAGIC was all over her when she walked into my office. It curled along the faded Oriental carpet, snagged on the dust bunnies under my desk, and crawled up the dark wood-paneled walls.

She settled into the worn leather chair across from me, tossed back her blonde pageboy and challenged me with her baby-blues.

She was trouble on two very shapely legs, and the sooner I got her out of my office the better. I didn't need any more trouble. Especially trouble that stank of magic.

Not that I couldn't use the work. The chipped gilt paint on the glass in the office door read "Les e Mess er, Invest ator." My name was Leslie Ann Messner—I'd dropped the "Ann" a long time ago—but I couldn't afford to repaint the door. Or replace the beat-up furniture. Hell, even the bottle in my desk drawer was definitely bottom-shelf hooch.

But magic? No thanks.

I should have told her to clear out. Shouldn't have let her open her mouth before I tossed her sweet little can out on the street.

I knew she'd make me regret it before I ever heard her tale. But I'm a sucker for a pretty face and a sob story, and she had both. In spades.

She told me her name was Laura Miller. Said her husband Sanford took her kid. She didn't know where, didn't know how. Just wanted the kid back, no questions asked.

I tried. Really, I did. I told her she wanted the cops, not a middle-aged broad with a bad attitude and a trick knee.

She was pretty and I knew she expected that to get her what she wanted, but truth be told, she wasn't really my type—I prefer my playmates with a little more heft to them, if you know what I mean.

"No police. I need you." Her tone left no room for argument. Or explanation. This was one dame who was used to getting her way.

Seamlessly shifting gears, Laura pulled out a dainty little hankie and dabbed at the tears that threatened to spill down her cheeks. "I just want my Joey back."

I had to hand it to her—she was good. The gesture didn't even look all that practiced.

She gave me pictures of Sanford and Joey, and wrote me a check I was pretty sure would bounce.

When Laura stood up she offered me her hand. "You will call me?" she asked, though it wasn't really a question.

I nodded and stood to take her hand. The soft skin was at odds with her callused fingertips. She drew her hand back, realizing I had noticed.

Her first mistake. Where did those calluses come from?

The stink of magic lingered after she left. It would be a long time before I got rid of it.

* * *

Streetlights flickered in the twilight, like lightning bugs in the gathering dusk. The address Laura gave me for Sanford's office was six long blocks uptown, just far enough to stretch my legs and kick-start my brain.

Thank God I was never one of those stilettos-and-pencil-skirt types. Brogans and wool slacks were better for walking, and nobody really noticed a woman my age if I didn't call attention to myself.

Sanford wouldn't be there. Laura swore he had disappeared three days ago, along with their four-year-old son, Joey.

If I believed her.

Sanford Miller's office building rose out of sight in the darkening sky. The ultra-modern façade and bronze-trimmed glass doors proclaimed its recent construction as clearly as the date chiseled in the lintel over the entrance.

At a desk just inside the door, a bored-looking security guard glanced up then looked away in dismissal.

I breathed deeply as I crossed the lobby. No magic here. If there was I'd smell it, like I had when Laura walked into my office.

I took the elevator to the 16th floor.

Through the open double doors opposite the elevator I could see a low, sleek desk with a tall, sleek woman seated behind it. On the wall behind starkly-modern cast bronze letters spelled out "Miller and Associates."

Mr. Miller, whatever he and his associated did, seemed to be pretty damned successful.

When I asked for Sanford Miller, the sleek woman gave me the once-over told me he was busy, and he wouldn't be available for the rest of the day.

"Can I leave him a note?"

She rolled her eyes, but said yes.

"Do you have some paper?"

Her lips flattened into a grim line and she handed me a sheet of thick, wheat-colored bond with the same logo as the letters on the wall.

I made a show of digging in my shoulder bag before I asked for a pen. The one she handed me had the company name and address printed on the barrel.

I fidgeted with the paper and pen, finally writing my name and number and the words "Call me" before folding the page in quarters. I leaned across the desk and pulled several long strips of tape from a dispenser, sealing the edges of the note as though it contained the secret of the universe.

The receptionist slid the taped-up bundle into a pigeon-hole on the wall below the bronze letters. The compartment was empty. Someone was picking up Sanford Miller's mail.

Somebody knew where he was.

The elevator doors opened. I nodded to the small man standing to one side and stepped in, reaching for the lobby button.

The smell hit me as soon as the doors closed. Magic. Strong magic.

I squared my shoulders and stared at the closed doors. Sixteen floors.

"Miller, eh?" The man said. He chuckled, a sound devoid of mirth.

I didn't respond, and he continued, speaking softly, as though to himself. "Looks like Sandy's done well for himself."

I grunted, a non-committal sound he could take as agreement if he wanted.

Apparently he did. He nodded in my direction. "Took some chances, but they paid off handsomely. Handsomely."

I was nearly choking on the stink of magic he had carried from the upper floors. He was the second person I'd encountered today, and I didn't believe in coincidence.

The source was in Sanford Miller's building, and I would have to find it.

I took a circuitous route from the lobby to the twentieth floor. I managed two flights of stairs before my knee forced me back to the elevator, but I didn't dare travel directly.

I rested in the stairwell on ten, and again at fifteen. Miller's was one flight up, and the man had come from above.

I climbed the last three flights slowly, resting at each landing, straining to hear if anyone entered the stairwell above me. As I climbed, the stink of magic grew stronger.

But when I opened the door to the twentieth floor, there was nothing to see. Blank doors. A window at the end of the corridor with a view of the alley.

And the stink of magic.

I made my way back to sixteen and checked Miller and Associates. Doors locked tight, lights off. No sign of anyone around.

Dead end.

I knew the answer was in that building, but I'd have to find it another way.

The pain in my knee killed any chance of walking home. I took a cab I couldn't afford back to the office, made dinner from the bottle in the desk drawer, and slept on the couch.

* * *

An old girl-friend worked the property records at City Hall. The break-up had been mutual, and she did me a favor now and then. I hoped this was one of those times.

Lucky for me, Teresa was in a good mood. All it took was a triple-shot mocha, and the building records appeared on the counter while the other clerk was on a break.

Convenient.

The interesting part was buried in the permit details: a residential occupancy permit for the top floor. Issued two weeks ago.

In the name of Sanford Miller.

He was hiding in plain sight.

* * *

I considered a dozen or more schemes to get in to see Sanford Miller, and discarded them all. Each more convoluted than the last, they were all doomed to failure.

In the end, I simply knocked on his door.

And the little man from the elevator answered.

"Wondered how long it would take you," he muttered as he swung the door wide. "You want to see Joey, right?"

I thought I'd been discreet, and my surprise must have shown on my face.

He barked a harsh laugh. "We figured she'd go to you, once everybody else turned her down." He gestured for me to follow him down a long hallway. "They did, you know. But we knew you'd fall for her—story."

He paused to be sure I caught his meaning. I did, but like I said before, she really wasn't my type. They didn't know me as well as they thought.

The hallway opened into an expansive living room, tastefully furnished, with a wall of windows overlooking the downtown streets. From twenty stories up the streets were ribbons of traffic glinting in the morning sun, and no noise reached us from below.

Sanford Miller sat on a leather sofa with his back to the windows, a newspaper abandoned on the low table in front of him.

"Remy said you'd show up."

I glanced down at my guide.

"Allow me to introduce you, Ms. Messner. This is Remy Peauride. Laura's older brother." He paused to let that sink in. "Joey's uncle."

I can't say I was surprised. Sure, the squat creature standing in front of me bore no obvious resemblance to the willowy woman who had hired me. But there was something about the eyes, something I hadn't seen the day before when I avoided looking at him.

He smelled of the same magic, only stronger.

"I imagine you want to see Joey," he continued, "and you will. But first I think we should have a little talk. Please, sit down."

It was a command, couched in the form of an invitation.

I'd deliberately walked into Sanford Miller's hiding place looking for answers, and it appeared he was willing to give me some.

I sat.

"I'll get right to the point, Ms. Messner." Miller leaned forward, his elbows resting on his knees. He was perfectly relaxed, at ease on his home turf, and I was the intruder.

I forced myself to lean back in my chair, feigning an air of nonchalance. "Please do."

"I know Laura is looking for us, for Joey. She will stop at nothing to take the boy away from me, but being here with me—with us—is what's best for the boy.

"It isn't as though he doesn't have any contact with Laura's family. He's extremely close to his uncle and Remy has offered to stay as long as he's needed. To help Joey, of course."

His voice was strong. Persuasive. He poured all the sincerity he could muster into each word. "I want what is best for Joey, and I can see that he gets it." He gestured toward a checkbook open on the table next to his newspaper.

"Whatever my wife—excuse me, my former wife— offered you, I can triple it." He arched an eyebrow and there was a twinkle of malicious glee as he continued. "And I can promise you my check won't bounce."

I kept my face impassive, but I was impressed. I'd already had a call from my bank this morning, warning me not to draw on the check I'd deposited. Sanford Miller clearly has his fingers in a lot of pies.

"All you have to do is tell her the truth. Tell her you saw the boy, he's healthy and happy. His uncle and I are taking good care of him.

"I haven't kidnapped my son, Ms. Messner. I have every legal right to have him with me.

"Convince Laura to drop this fool's errand and the money is yours."

He hadn't allowed me to speak as he presented his offer. Now he sat back and cocked his head. It was my turn.

I paused to consider my next move. Both Millers told convincing tales, and I suspected there was a kernel of truth is each one. The question was which tale I chose to believe.

Before I could answer, Remy returned. He carried a tray with a silver coffee service, and was accompanied by a child nearly as tall as he was.

I recognized Joey from the picture Laura had given me. It was obviously a recent one—children change quickly at that age.

What the photo hadn't shown was how closely his eyes resembled Laura's. And Remy's.

As the child drew closer my nose was assaulted by the stink of magic. Not like what I smelled on Laura, or even the thick stench in the elevator.

My head swam and my eyes filled with water. This was magic more powerful than anything I had ever experienced, and it was coming from a child of four.

Remy nodded at me as he set the coffee service on the table and poured. He handed me a steaming cup. "Drink. It will help."

The two men waited while I sipped the pungent brew. The sharp taste of chicory and the mossy flavor of chamomile battled with the strong coffee in an unpleasant cacophony—but it muted the stench.

Joey offered me a plate of pastries. I took one, though I wasn't keen on actually eating it.

"Thanks, kid."

"You're welcome." He studied my face for a minute, then shrugged and turned to Sanford. "Can I go play now?"

Sanford looked at me quizzically. I shook my head. There wasn't anything to see, and I sure wasn't getting any secrets out of the kid with his dad and uncle in the room.

"Sure, sport. We'll have breakfast in a little while. Okay?"

Joey nodded and trotted away without a backward glance.

"Now you understand." Sanford Miller pinned me with his eyes. "You see why he can't go back to that woman. She can't be trusted with him."

It seemed to me there were several people that couldn't be trusted with the child, but this wasn't the time or the place to tell him that.

"You also should understand that we will not be here, should you choose to return with my former wife. Our documents are in order, we can travel at a moment's notice, and we will know if you're coming."

I didn't doubt that last. Sanford Miller had easily demonstrated the speed and scope of his information-gathering. He was well-connected and he had eyes everywhere.

Sanford held all the cards.

"My sister," Remy spoke for the first time since he'd shown me into the room, "has no appreciation for the challenges of raising a child like Joey. I, on the other hand, have trained for years for just such a possibility. I recognize the boy's potential—for good, or ill."

They'd made their pitch, and delivered the thinly-veiled threats. There was nothing more for me to do.

"I'll speak to my client," I assured them. "But I doubt it will do any good. In one short interview I realized she is someone who is used to getting things her way, and you two should know that far better than I."

Sanford Miller smiled. That is to say, he lifted the corners of his mouth in the approximation of a conspiratorial grin. I felt like he should be displaying rows of tiny shark teeth, and it sent a chill down my spine.

"I know you can be very persuasive, Ms. Messner. I'm sure none of us want this to go any further. Don't you agree?"

"Of course."

Remy took my empty cup and put it on the coffee tray. "I'll show you out."

When the door closed behind me I had the distinct impression that the room would simply not be there if I opened the door again.

Superstitious? Maybe. But out in the hall again I couldn't smell even a whiff of magic.

* * *

Laura, as predicted, did not take the news well.

"Take me to him," she demanded, refusing to accept my explanation that Joey, Remy and Sanford would not be found unless they wanted to be.

I told her what I had seen, and what I was told. "The boy is fine," I said, hoping it was true.

"He's not fine. I know it." Her eyes filled with tears, and genuine emotion thickened her voice. "I've been there," she added softly.

"You think I married Sanford for his money, don't you?" She laughed harshly. "It was the other way around. I didn't actually have money," she went on, "but I could make it.

"Remember the old story about the girl who made gold from straw? That was me."

I shook my head. "Old wives tale."

"The straw part, sure. But the rest? I could pick investments. Not 100%, but 90-plus. Sanford had a little money. He realized I could turn it into a lot, very quickly, and I did.

"Word got around, but like any good story it got retold and embellished and exaggerated. People didn't want to believe a girl could do that, so they gave Remy credit. You know how that is?"

I nodded.

"I didn't care. In fact, it was easier if no one knew it was me. Nobody bothered me. Sanford was happy, and everything seemed great until I got pregnant with Joey."

She pulled a worn photograph from her purse and handed it to me. Her and Sanford, grinning at each other so hard it looked like their faces would break. Hard to believe they were the same two people I was dealing with now.

"That's the day we found out about Joey. A couple weeks later I started making mistakes. Little ones at first, then bigger ones. It was the hormones. Sanford let everything coast, figuring I'd be back to normal after the baby was born.

"I wasn't."

She slipped the photo back in her purse. "Sanford should have been fine without my help by then. He had plenty of money and the business was successful. Everyone was happy but Remy."

I felt my resolve slipping. I knew we'd lost, Sanford and Remy had what they wanted and we were powerless to fight them. Still, Laura's story was drawing me into her world; into a place I didn't want to go.

"The power had transferred to Joey. Not all of it, but a lot, even though he was too young to do anything with it.

"That's when Remy moved in. He kept at Sanford about all the things Joey could do if we just trained him properly. He finally convinced Sanford, and they shut me out.

"That crack Remy made about taking chances? The only chance they took was to get their investment advice from a two-year-old!" She was genuinely angry now, the power of her emotions filling the office. "Even worse, it worked."

She pulled herself to her feet. "I'm going over there. I know I can't fight Sanford's connections and Remy's power, but I have to try. I have to do something!"

What can I say? I'm a sucker for a sob story, but I'm an even bigger sucker for lost causes. Probably why I started doing this job in the first place.

I was out the door and down the block, matching her long legs stride for stride. We covered the six blocks in record time and swept into the lobby of Sanford's office building.

The elevator ride to the top floor took forever. With each floor I sniffed for a trace of magic, but all I could smell was the faded power within Laura. No Remy. No Joey.

The doors opened on twenty, and I turned down the corridor toward the door to Sanford's penthouse. It stood open, the empty space beyond ending in blank walls blocking out the daylight.

No windows. No view. No carpets or furniture.

And no Joey.

We haven't given up exactly. The odds are long, but we follow every item on the financial pages.

One day, we'll find him. Until then, we just keep looking.

Cupid's Crib

Cupid's Crib

"THEY DON'T WANT IT." Coop slouched against his desk, a stocking cap pulled low over his tightly-curled dark hair, a sneer twisting his full lips. "I'm tellin' you, Allie, these jive-ass people do not want true love."

Allie, her shift in the love boutique over, settled into the worn sofa Coop kept against the opposite wall. Her mouth lifted in a tired, resigned smile that quickly disappeared. This was their nightly ritual, her and Coop. Going over the day's receipts, and having this argument.

Coop popped the top of a tall boy, and glared at her, daring her to say anything. He was a walking cliché, but there wasn't anything she could say that would make him change his behavior. Rather, he relished his persona as a disaffected black man, even though she knew differently. She knew how much they pulled down every day, and she had seen the elegant townhouse Coop called home. Still, he put on the attitude, and tonight she was too tired to give him the fight he so obviously relished.

But somehow she couldn't stop herself. "You are so full of shit," she said. "No wonder your eyes are brown."

Coop rolled his dark eyes, and shook his head. "Didn't nobody tell you it ain't a good career move to dis your boss like that, girl? It's trash talk like that gets a person fired."

Allie smiled, for real this time. "Yeah, right. Like I don't tell you that most every day. And it's not like you've got people beating down the door to work for you. Not after the last three clerks you chased off."

Coop shrugged elaborately. "I could find me another 'retail manager,' Miss High-and-Mighty. I could find me another manager in a heartbeat, and you'd be out on your sweet little ass."

"You know, Coop," Allie sat up, putting her feet flat on the floor. "There are still sexual harassment laws in this country. You aren't supposed to talk to me like that."

"Aw, girl, you know I'm just kidding." His voice dropped into an attempt at sweet-talk, though it came out more like a whine. "And that is a sweet little ass you got there."

Allie laughed. "Coop, you are still full of shit, and I am still tired. I am gonna show you my sweet little ass, going out the door." Her actions followed her words, and she walked out of the office.

Pulling her keys from her purse, she called back over her shoulder. "I'll see you in the morning, Coop. Don't piss off any customers in the meantime, okay?"

She walked out the door, bolting it behind her, and walked past the display windows, with their array of lingerie and lotions. The loopy script that spelled out "Cupid's Crib" across the window was so brilliant pink that it nearly glowed in the streetlights on the deserted sidewalk. Coop would go out the back, and check the lock there before he left. It was part of their comfortable pattern, the rituals they had developed in the six years she had worked for him.

Didn't seem that long, though. Allie walked toward the El, shrugging off the uneasy feeling she got when she thought about Coop. She didn't want to examine the reasons she stayed at a job with a sexist, foul-mouthed poser.

She told herself it was because she knew he was a poser. He wasn't any of the things he claimed to be, although she supposed the black part was for real. You couldn't hardly fake that, could you? Then again, if he was really Cupid, as he claimed he was, maybe he could.

She gave a harsh little laugh as she boarded the nearly-empty train. God of Love, my sweet little ass. More like the God of Bad Attitude. She just hoped he wouldn't open early tomorrow, and scare away the customers before she got there.

He'd done that a couple times lately. Scared customers away. Most of the time it was okay, he stayed in the back, behind the one-way mirror behind the register, and left her alone. But once in a while, when he was in a particularly foul mood, he'd come out, and "help" her with a customer.

Mostly, his help meant bad-mouthing the customer's choice of goods, and harassing them about why they had come in his shop. Sometimes, they got angry, and told him they had no idea why they had come in, since he was so obnoxious, and stormed out. It lost Coop a sale, which he richly deserved, but it also lost Allie a tiny piece of her profit-sharing, and that pissed her off.

But the worst were the women, mostly women anyway, who cried. After Coop yelled, and badgered, and asked questions that were really none of his business, after he stalked back into his office, dismissing the customer, and her concerns—then came the tears.

They always had a reason to be there, which usually boiled down to, "If I can just make him love me," and the fact that it was weak and pathetic didn't make it any less sad. And she didn't need to see sad. She'd seen enough of that already.

Working at Cupid's Crib wasn't all bad. Really. She made enough money to afford a condo within walking distance of the El, and a red convertible, the kind her mom had called a "zip-zap" car. She kept the Miata garaged most of the time, preferring the convenience of the train, but a drive along Lake Michigan was a sweet reward on her rare days off.

And it wasn't just the money. She wanted to help people find love, and if the potions and lotions and candles she sold helped them, that was good enough for her.

* * *

By morning, her argument with Coop was old history, as it was every morning. She unlocked the front door, booted up the cash register system, ran a stock report, and put it on Coop's desk. He did most of the ordering, since he usually didn't insult the suppliers.

As she waited, watching the early shoppers stroll through Enchantment Place, eyeing the shop windows and occasionally venturing inside one shop or another, she worried about Coop.

He had been getting worse, she was forced to admit. It had happened slowly, almost imperceptibly, but she had noticed. Maybe his attitude problem was *his* problem, and none of her business, but if it drove away enough customers, it would become her problem, too. And that made it her business.

Not that she gave a damn, if Coop wanted to act like a jerk. Let him. Just don't destroy Cupid's Crib in the process, that was all.

But what if there was a way, some way to convince him that people *did* want true love? Would that change his attitude? Probably not. Coop seemed real fond of his attitude problem.

The thought continued to nag at the back of her brain all day. Coop stayed out of the way, dealing with suppliers, she waited on customers, and at day's end Allie still hadn't made a decision.

At least, not a conscious one.

But when Coop started his usual rant after running the totals for the day, Allie took a different approach.

"Why do you say that, Coop?" she asked earnestly, her eyes begging him for an honest answer. "Really. You give me some jive-ass answer about how people want an easy out, they don't want real love, but you have never given me a real answer about why you feel that way."

She looked him over, waiting for an answer—baggy pants slopping over his expensive sneakers, flashy gold jewelry, the permanent sneer that curled his mouth—his costume was a part of the attitude, and as far as she was concerned, it was time for a major change.

"Girl," Coop said, "that ain't none of your business."

"You made it my business when you started driving away customers, Coop. Look at today's totals," she pointed at the reports spread across his desk. "Then look at last Tuesday, the day you decided to help out front. We lost, what, thirty percent of the sales that day?"

Coop raised his hands on mock surrender. "So, I should stay out of the store. I'm down with that, okay?"

"Not okay. You promise that every time, and every time you end up back out there, bad-mouthing a customer, making trouble. You make people *cry* out there."

"It says 'Cupid' on the door, girl, not 'stupid.' People gotta know when it says Cupid, it means love. But no! They're all up in my face, saying they want to meet somebody, but what they really want is to score, to get lucky."

"You really believe that, Coop? Do you?" Allie thrust her chin out, challenging Coop. "Care to put your money where your mouth is?"

Coop slouched behind his desk, and dropped heavily into his chair. "Money ain't no big thing. I got enough. And you do, too."

"I won't have for long, if you keep going the way you do." Allie's irritation boiled over, and she sprang to her feet, pacing in front of the desk, her hands balled into fists. "I mean it, Coop. I've had it with your attitude. I can't take it any more." She stopped, planting her fists on the desktop and leaning over, getting in Coop's face. "Serious. Dead serious. This shit has got to stop."

He looked up at her, feigning boredom. She knew better, knew he was masking his true feelings, but she couldn't get through to him. But as she stared him down, she saw a subtle shift, a chink in his mask. For an instant, she saw fear, and hesitation.

"So, what's it going to take?" she said quietly, pressing her advantage. "What if I prove to you that people want love, would that make any difference in your crap-ass attitude?"

He relaxed, the fear replaced by arrogance. He laughed, a harsh, hard sound. "You can try, girl, but no way can you prove it, 'cause it's not true. No way, no how. Nobody wants the real thing. It's too messy, too hard, and too damned much work."

Coop stood up, straightening from his usual slouch to tower over her. At six-foot-five, and whip-slender, he was an imposing figure, but she wasn't going to be intimidated. She held his gaze, leaning her head back to maintain eye contact.

When he continued his voice was soft, and sad. The brittle shell had been pierced for a moment, and he looked steadily into her eyes. "I've been doing this job for hundreds, no, thousands, of years, girl. I've offered mortals love again and again and again, only to have them throw it away, in search of—something. I could give you a list—Henry the Eighth, just as an example. There's true love out there," he gestured through the one-way window, into the store, "but I guaran-damn-tee you, nobody's gonna buy it."

"If it's out there," she replied, "where is it? Which bottle? Which jar?"

"If somebody wants it, it'll turn up." Coop's harsh laugh returned. "But ain't nobody going to want it."

* * *

Allie began her campaign the next morning. With each customer, she made an extra effort, offered a little more. By two o'clock, she was exhausted, and beginning to think Coop was right. They all wanted the sizzle, but nobody wanted more.

She was straightening incense and candles, not looking for anything special, not really. Just cleaning up, making the place inviting, when she spotted a little heart-shaped candle she didn't think she'd seen before.

Her heart leaped, in spite of herself. Maybe this was the thing Coop had talked about. And if it had appeared, then the customer that wanted it would be the next one.

She watched the door expectantly, waiting for the person who would prove Coop wrong, who would force his to reconsider his bad attitude. But when the sensor on the door beeped, it was a hard-looking thirty-something woman, and she was in a hurry.

"Music?" she asked brusquely. "Something kind of, you know, sexy."

A few minutes later, she left, clutching a CD of Ravel's *Bolero* and assuring Allie it was exactly what she wanted. Allie didn't have the heart to tell her she was a walking cliché, and any man who responded to such an obvious ploy wasn't worth the effort.

She looked at the candle, sitting on the counter, abandoned while she rang up *Bolero*-woman's CD. She shrugged, and shoved it under the counter. She'd have to find the manifest, and get a proper price on it before she put it back on the shelf.

The phone beeped, and Allie picked up the inside line.

"It's not the candle," Coop said, from the other side of the window. "That came in last week, must have lost the price sticker. Five-ninety-nine, if you want to put it back in its place. And true love? I'm telling you, nobody wants it."

Two days later, she once again thought she'd found her chance. An older couple, well past retirement age, came through the front door, hand-in-hand. The woman reddened as she looked over the array of merchandise, and her companion seemed flustered. But they exchanged a glance, and approached Allie.

She smiled at the woman, trying to put her at ease. Cupid's Crib could be a little daunting the first time you came in. Allie noticed that neither the man nor the woman wore a wedding ring, and the woman quickly stuck her left hand in the pocket of her sweater when she caught Allie's glance.

It was sweet, really. Love could find you any time, at any age. Allie remembered of the rose-scented lotion she had stocked earlier that morning. It seemed like just the right thing for such a sweet couple.

The man moved a few steps away, leaving Allie with the blushing woman. Allie smiled again, and said, in her sweetest voice, "Can I help you?"

The woman hesitated, and Allie went into her sales pitch. "I know this can be a little overwhelming, the first time you come in. We have so many lovely things! But perhaps if you give me some idea what you're looking for…?" Her voice trailed off delicately, inviting the woman to share the secret longing that had brought her through the door.

"I don't know if you can help me, dear. I'm not even quite sure why we came in here. But I suppose you might have something," she turned her head, taking in the shelves of lotions, and racks of lacy gowns and robes. She continued to turn, looking toward the back of the shop, where the naughtier merchandise lurked, away from the casual glance of a passer-by, and blushed again.

Allie touched her arm, and steered her toward the lotion display, away from the back of the shop. She put a drop of the rose lotion on the woman's hand. "Very smooth and silky," Allie said, "makes your skin soft and so touchable."

The woman hesitated, glancing back at her companion with a fond smile. He was engrossed in a display of videos, and already had a couple in his hand, Allie noticed.

"You're a lucky woman," Allie said. "To have someone you care about so much."

The woman sighed, and moved toward the register, the lotion in her hand. "I suppose." She turned her back to the man, and dropped her voice to a whisper. "I just wish he'd go ahead and propose already. I know he wants to, and I am sure as hell tired of trying to live on a single pension. When we're married," her whisper carried a tone of desperation, "at least we'll only have one household to support."

"But you love him, don't you. I can see it," Allie insisted.

"Maybe." The woman shrugged. "Doesn't matter. We need each other, and that has to be enough."

"I might be able to help you." An idea took hold of Allie. If the woman just said she *wanted* love, then the thing, whatever it was, would appear. That's what Coop had said.

The woman shook her head. "Tried that once, didn't work out so well. What we have is fine." She looked over at her companion, who had turned her direction. "You about ready, Norman?"

"Right there, honey," he replied. He glanced down at the videos in his hand, then set them back on the rack with a shrug. "Ready whenever you are."

The couple left the store, holding hands, the small plastic bag with the lotion bottle tucked carefully in the bottom of the woman's handbag.

Strike two.

* * *

"Admit it," Coop said, smirking. "You can't find anybody says they really want true love. You've been trying with every customer." He nodded toward the window. "I can see you, all day, trying to convince people, but you got no takers."

It had been a long day, a typically busy Saturday. Lots of twenty-somethings in pairs and packs, looking for an edge for their Saturday nights. Quartets of thirty-somethings, fueled by reruns of *Sex and the City* and a couple round of pomegranate cosmos, trying to convince themselves they were hip and happening.

And not a one of them had asked for love. They asked for sexy lingerie, spicy cologne, scented candles, bubble bath, body paint, and bath oils. The cosmo-driven career women dared each other to try on the skimpiest lingerie, and shrieked about how this boyfriend of that husband would react. They even bought love potions, which Allie knew were mostly sugar water and food coloring. But nobody asked if they really worked. They didn't want to know.

Late in the afternoon, Coop wandered out into the front. He sauntered up and down the aisles, looking at the displays, occasionally rearranging merchandise, or stopping at a discreet distance to listen to customers discussing their purchases.

Allie held her breath, waiting for the chaos that would inevitably follow. He was going to wreak havoc, he couldn't help it. She just didn't know what form it would take today.

But instead he wandered back to the office.

It was nearly closing time when he emerged, and she could feel his attitude from across the shop. There weren't any customers, and he stalked up and down the aisles, as though looking for something to complain about.

Allie considered flipping the "OPEN" sign over and locking the door, pretending that it was time to close. But she knew she couldn't get away with it. Coop would not only notice, he'd badger her about losing business, turning her own arguments about lost sales back against her.

She eyed the clock warily, as Coop continued his inspection. Fifteen minutes to closing time, maybe eleven or twelve until she could lock the door with a clear conscience.

It wasn't to be.

The door buzzed, and Allie hurried to wait on the man who walked in. But she wasn't fast enough. Coop got there first, greeting the guy like he was an old friend, though it was clear they had never laid eyes on each other before. Still, the guy responded with the same show of camaraderie.

The two men moved toward the back of the store, where the raunchiest merchandise lurked in subdued lighting. Their laughter drifted back to her, a sound that made her feel as though she needed a shower.

The man made his selections quickly. As he approached the counter, Coop caught Allie's eye, and motioned forcefully for her to come over and handle the register. He was grinning in triumph, confident of his victory.

Dismay flooded through Allie as she bagged the toys and lubricants. He leered at her as she rang up the merchandise, wagging his eyebrows in what she supposed was meant to be a suggestive manner.

"Sure you don't want to join my little party?" he asked, as she took his credit card. "Platinum card means never having to say 'No,'" he added, as though that made him something special.

Allie's stomach churned, but she forced a polite smile. "Sorry," she said. "I never socialize with the customers. It's kind of a store policy."

A policy that she had instituted in the last fifteen seconds, and which caused Coop's eyebrows to lift in surprise. The accompanying grin told her he could barely contain his glee at her response.

The customer took her rejection with poor grace, trying to insist that he was different, that she should break her policy "just this once" for him. It took her another ten minutes of increasingly adamant refusals before she could get him out the door.

As she swung the door behind him, he turned around and threw her a kiss. "You don't know what you're missing," he said.

Allie slammed the door. "Oh, yes. I think I do know," she muttered. "I think I know all too well."

Across the shop, Coop was practically vibrating. His eyes were bright, and his straight, white teeth showed against his dark skin in a wide smile.

"Give it up, girl. I'm right. I am sooo right. There isn't even a word for how right I am. Admit it, now." He shook his head, and the diamond stud in his ear caught the light, twinkling at her. Even his *jewelry* was mocking her.

"You think he was looking for love, Allie? Think that stuff was to help him find true love?" Coop's laughter spiraled up, bordering on hysteria. "You think that was about love? The guy wanted a lot of things, girl, and he was pretty clear about what they were, and not a one of them came anywhere near love."

Anger flashed over Allie. She felt the heat climb through her body, flowing through her arms and legs, spreading outward from her core.

Her vision narrowed, until all she could see was Coop's mouth, his lips and tongue laughing and mocking. There was no sign, no hint, of the man she once though lived inside that shell, the man behind the mask.

He'd gone too far.

She started across the shop. She had to stop him, stop the laughter. If she couldn't break through, couldn't get through to him, then she was done. Her profit-sharing, her condo, her zip-zap car, none of it was worth the pain that stabbed at her heart and blurred her vision with tears.

As she walked toward Coop, not knowing what she would do when she reached him, she brushed her hand along a counter of decorations.

Instinctively, she grabbed a dusty plastic toy that threatened to fall off the shelf. It was a miniature bow and arrow, a cheap plastic imitation of Cupid's traditional weapon, that had been placed on a clearance rack months earlier. But no one wanted it, and it had been pushed aside many times, until her unintentional touch had pushed it over the edge.

Holding the bow, with the arrow dangling loosely from the string, she planted herself in front of Coop, craning her neck to look up at him.

"Stop!" she commanded.

He paused to look at her, surprise at her harsh tone registering on his face. He tried to hold back his laughter, biting his full lips in an effort to appease her.

"That's it, Coop. I quit. I can't take any more of your shit, and I can't stick around her and watch you destroy this place, and yourself."

She shoved the bow and arrow against his chest and let go. It snagged on one of his chains, and he reached up to yank it free.

As he did, the plastic tip of the arrow nicked his finger, drawing a tiny drop of blood.

Well, that was really it. Not only had she quit, she'd managed to injure Coop before she could get out the door. Now she was done for sure. Allie whirled around and grabbed her purse from under the register. She could send for her final check, and anything else she'd left behind.

She ran for the door without looking back. She'd seen enough of Coop's triumphant smirk, heard enough laughter to last her forever.

But before she could open the door, a hand closed over her arm, gently pulling her back, and turning her around.

Coop looked down at her. The laughter was gone, his eyes were wide, as he stared at her in amazement. There was a spot of blood on his shirt, and the bow and arrow were still tangled in his gold chains.

He looked from her to the arrow, and back again, as though he couldn't quite grasp what had happened. Then a slow grin broke over his face.

"Allie," he said, "do you believe in true love?"

About the Author

CHRISTINA F. YORK has always loved words, in every form. Her first foray into publishing, as the ten-year-old reporter, editor, and publisher of a one-page neighborhood newspaper, lasted only a few weeks. During the enforced retirement that followed, she finished grade school, high school, and college; married, had a couple kids, divorced, and re-married; and eventually found her way back to writing.

An Oregon native, Christina has always lived on the West Coast. After growing up in the suburbs of L.A., she spent many years in and around Seattle; moved to Eugene, Oregon; and eventually settled on the rugged Oregon coast, where she can see the ocean from her office window. She shares her home with her husband, writer J. Steven York, and a couple of very spoiled cats.